MURDER
BOY

MURDER BOY

Bryon Quertermous

Copyright © 2015 by Bryon Quertermous
Cover and jacket design by Adrijus Guscia
Interior designed and formatted by E.M. Tippetts Book Designs

ISBN 978-1-940610-27-6
eISBN 978-1-940610-46-7

First trade paperback edition March 2015 by Polis Books, LLC
1201 Hudson Street
Hoboken, NJ 07030
www.PolisBooks.com

POLIS BOOKS

To my uncle, John Merkel. He gave me my first typewriter and my first crime novel. This is all his fault.

CHAPTER 1

On the Saturday night before Christmas, after the creative writing department holiday party, I showed up for the second time at a warehouse store on the outskirts of Detroit drunk on cheap scotch and self-righteous bullshit looking to buy supplies for a kidnapping. It was ten minutes until closing time and I was telling the wide checkout girl in the wide orange apron about my fictional dog.

"Got the bladder of a senile old man," I said.

"Poor thing," she said.

"The plastic is for the carpet, to protect it. Not to wrap his dead body in or anything. I didn't kill him."

The cashier frowned and kept her eyes on me as she scanned the plastic. I looked longingly behind the cashier at the self-scan checkout already closed for the evening, wishing I could have avoided this whole person-to-person aspect completely.

"Seems like later at night like this they'd want to keep the self-scan open and close up these manned stations," I said, trying to change the subject.

"Well, Dominick, then I wouldn't have a job. I like my job. My daughter likes my job."

Shit. This was how it started at the party. Simple comment, botched context, swift descent into madness.

"I'm sorry," I said. "I didn't mean to…wait, how do you know my name?"

I had explicitly avoided using anything that could be traced back to me and had even passed up the 5% discount I could get as a rewards member to maintain my anonymity.

She pointed to my shirt and I looked down at the name tag everyone had been forced to wear at the party.

"What kind of dog did you say you had again?"

You'd think this would have set off alarms that maybe I was in over my head, but believe it or not, this was the smart part of my plan. Half an hour earlier I almost went through the same checkout occupied by the same checkout girl with a cart full of items—plastic sheets, rope, knives, and duct tape— that might as well have been packaged as a kidnapping value pack.

I'd thought about adding more items to make it all look less nefarious, but the last of my teaching stipend had gone to cover a bad night at the casino during a failed "research trip" for a heist novel I wanted to write. There was barely enough in my bank account to cover the essentials, so I put back everything except the plastic and initiated the charming commentary on my imaginary dog's bladder adventures.

There wasn't another flash of common sense until I stood outside The Professor's back door, three 24-hour store visits later, holding the plastic under my arm while trying not to drop the knife or the rope. The element of surprise I'd been hoping for quickly turned to the element of boredom when The Professor still hadn't returned home after almost half an hour. My adrenaline was starting to wear off and the booze was starting to set in, and if I waited too much longer I was afraid I'd fall asleep.

Then I remembered why I was there in the first place, why I drank cheap scotch instead of the 20 year-old Macallan that had been making the rounds.

The Professor—Parker Farmington, Adjunct Assistant Professor, MFA East Ass End of Nowhere U—had refused to sign off on my final novel project, jeopardizing my second chance fellowship in New York City. Without the fellowship I'd have no other choice but to work the midnight shift at some godforsaken truck stop along I-75, destined to be shot to death by an angry trucker or a skittish hooker, a box full of unfinished manuscripts and second rate online publications as my final legacy.

The only other place The Professor could be was Posey Wade's house. She and The Professor had been flirting and touching the whole time at the party. Nobody was officially supposed to know they were together, but it was common knowledge in the department. Posey was one of the better writers in the workshop and we shared a passion for Michael Chabon and *The Simpsons*. I'd been to her house in the student ghetto near the campus a few times and was pretty sure I could find my way back, even buzzed. It was a neighborhood where one wouldn't particularly stick out walking down the street carrying plastic and rope.

• • •

BY THE time I reached Posey's house, I'd re-run my last encounter with The Professor at the party until my rage supplanted the alcohol-induced lethargy threatening to derail my plan. It started toward the end of the party during a conversation about movies, one of Farmington's favorite topics as well as one of my own, and I was looking for a scrap of conversation that I hoped could turn into a discussion about my novel.

But The Professor quickly spun the conversation toward a short story I wrote that included a snippet of screenplay format to show a character reliving a painful experience. I made things worse by trying to defend myself and mentioning the story had gone on to be published in a respected crime fiction journal and shortlisted for —

"Respected online crime journal," Farmington said.

"Like a whore with morals," a slicing blonde literature professor said.

"Or a pedophile who tithes," a lumpy black essay lecturer

said.

Farmington then took the opportunity to bring the story up on one of the library computer with a giant monitor so everyone could see it and my accompanying author photo where I was holding an old-school Nintendo video gun with the cord dangling seductively from my mouth. It wasn't long after that someone printed the story and began an impromptu live reading that devolved into a Rocky Horror Picture Show-style assault on every piece of the story.

Then the cheap scotch.

Then the trip to the home improvement store.

Then the cashier with the apron.

Then the dog.

Etc.

My plan outside of Posey's house was slightly more developed than the previous incarnation, but it was all for naught because the first person I saw was Posey Wade sitting in a hot tub and she told me Farmington was already gone.

"Did you need to see him about something?" She asked.

"Kidnapping," I said. "Wait, no. I mean it's about my thesis."

"You have plastic, and what appears to be rope."

"Why are you in a hot tub? It's freezing out."

"It's invigorating; the mix of hot and cold. Also, I think one of the girls who lives here does a nude webcam to pay her rent and we sure as hell don't want that *inside* the house."

"Right. You wrote a story about that for workshop," I

said. "It would have made a great crime story."

"Some of the other students, not me because I like you and your writing, they call you Murder Boy because you always kill people off in your stories, even the romantic ones."

"You like me?"

If I'd had a tail, it would have been wagging then with eager thoughts of Posey's approval of my life choices. Maybe she'd scratch my ears, or suck my —

"Sure. You have a great voice and your characters are always a riot. Your dialogue is some of the best I've ever heard."

And then I felt as deflated as the bladder of the dog I'd made up earlier. I was drunk enough where the pee I felt running down my leg could have been literal rather than metaphorical.

"Oh, you like me as a writer."

"I mean it's not real dialogue, like how people speak in real life, but in real life people are boring and say 'um' a lot."

"Were you in the hot tub with Professor Farmington?"

"Ah…"

"Everybody knows you two are together. You should embrace it."

"It's complicated."

"So he's not here, then, right?"

"No. He screwed me then left me like he always does. Just once I want to stay over at his house. It's a nice house."

"I just came from there," I said, holding up the plastic

and the rope. "He won't sign my thesis."

"Are you still drunk from the party?"

"Sort of. I think there was something wacky in the punch."

"You don't look good. Come sit in here with me and relax."

"You're going to tattle on me, on what I was planning."

"Come here. You really look like you could use —"

"I'm just frustrated. I wasn't really going to do anything, and even if I wanted to I can't pull something like that off. But he's just such a...I mean since I've known him he's always —"

"Are you crying?"

"This is my future he's screwing with."

"I'd come out and hug you or something for comfort," Posey said, "but I don't have any clothes on."

"Ew," I said. "Why are you naked in the porn tub?"

"I, uh, I tend to throw my clothes when I'm really getting into it."

She pointed toward various pieces of clothing spread across the yard and in the tree next to the hot tub.

"Should I take off my clothes?" I asked.

"See, that's why I like you. That sounds like something one of your characters would say."

I laughed and stripped down to my boxer briefs, but paused before removing them. I've never been a prude and have what some may determine is a socially backward lack of shame in my body, but the last thing I needed was

Farmington coming back and catching me naked in the hot tub with his girlfriend. I'd be forced to defend myself naked and whether I won or lost, it wouldn't matter; this was my life with Parker Farmington. Even if I screwed his mistress, he'd still win and *I'd* be screwed

"Are you sure this okay? I mean will—"

"Come on already," she said. "The heater's on the fritz in here and the water is starting to cool off. I could use another body."

If I really was going to be stuck in Detroit with a dead-end job for the rest of my life, this could be the last chance a naked woman would ever invite me into her hot tub without charging me. So I stripped off the underwear, shoved any thoughts of how many amateur porn stars had preceded me in the hot tub, and climbed in next to Posey. She reached over the side of the hot tub and came up with two cans of beer.

"Now let's keep that buzz going while you tell me about this kidnapping plan of yours."

CHAPTER
2

I woke up the next morning still wet, but not in the hot tub. It took several minutes for my brain to reactivate from whatever shut it down and acclimate to its current surroundings. I soon realized I wasn't back at my place and that the wet feeling probably had something to do with the guy standing over me with a spray bottle.

"I use it on the cats," the man said. "They're pretty dumb but this still gets them off the couch. But you…"

There was something about the voice I recognized, but I couldn't quite place it. I tried to latch onto what I last remembered. The party, the home improvement store, oh yeah, the hot tub. There was a girl. Shit. This was probably her boyfriend. Wait. The girl was from my class. Oh shit. Her boyfriend was —

"Professor," I said. "What are you doing here? I mean, wait, this isn't your house is it?"

"There's coffee in the kitchen. Your clothes are on the floor here next to you. They smell like vomit but I don't think the washer here works."

I sat up and felt around for my clothes, trying to figure out how to play this. But my head was barely ready to process standard movement and anti-vomit commands, let alone create complex scene reconstructions from the night before and place them in a context in which I'd be comfortable making my next move.

In fact, my brain only seemed to be able to focus on one task at a time and when pulling on my shirt and pants became the prime focus, the anti-vomit walls went down. I threw up all over the inside of my shirt, and while trying to remove the vomit shirt, the rest of my body gave up its fight against gravity and collapsed in a pile between Posey and Farmington. Posey squatted next to me and helped me squirm out of my vomit shirt.

"I was telling Parker about our conversation last night," she said.

Oh?

"Oh?"

That didn't have to mean anything. Posey and Farmington probably talked about a lot of things. They shared many of the same interests and some common acquaintances.

"I was telling him about your plan," she continued.

Oh. Shit.

"Really?" I asked. "Why would you do that?"

"It certainly impacts him, don't you think?"

"Uh..."

There was no way to know what Posey already told Farmington. In the sober light of day it was easier to believe Posey could be setting me up than it was that she was my new muse or possible wealthy patron. So maybe I should just say as little as possible and wait and see what happened. Yeah, that seemed like a good plan. And it worked until I got to the kitchen, looking for something starchy to help me regain my inner balance, and heard Posey talking.

"Go ahead and explain it to him. Maybe he has some ideas for better execution."

That definitely sounded like she was setting him up, but all he could do was stumble along the conversational mine field until he figured out an escape route or blew himself up.

"I was drunk," I said. "You say things when you're drunk that—"

"You peed off most of your buzz by the time we ended up in bed. It was a good plan. Tell him."

My head was starting to spin now. Confusion and panic were adding to my hangover and paranoia.

"What? Bed? Did we—"

"No. We watched TV and I kicked you to the couch when you kept snoring. Now tell him the plan."

"That's really not a good idea."

"See, I told you," Farmington said. "He's all talk and bravado in workshop but when given a legitimate chance to do something with his work, he crumbles into a—"

"You really want to hear this?" I asked. "I don't get it. What are you trying to do to me?"

"To you? I want to do this *for* you," Posey said.

I took the insulated Disney princess mug of coffee Posey offered me and sat down at the kitchen table. The kitchen was the oldest part of an old house occupied mostly by students without the skill or desire to provide proper upkeep. The chair wobbled when I sat down and it was enough of a jolt to make me wonder if, instead of hung over, I was still drunk.

"Let's say we do this," I said. "How do you suggest we start?"

What was I even saying? Why would Farmington be part of his own kidnapping? They had to have an angle and damned if I couldn't figure out what it was. I needed to get out of there and get my head clear and see if I could shake anything helpful loose on my own turf.

"I have to go to work," Farmington finally said. "Maybe you two can—"

"Tell him about the first story," Posey said. "The one you told me last night. You know, Murder Boy."

"Story?"

"For the collection. You know. For your thesis."

"Ohhhhhh. My thesis. I thought you were talking about the other thing."

The dominos were beginning to fall and I could feel clouds lifting from my head as the file drawers in my brain that had been knocked loose slid back into place. We were talking about writing, not kidnapping. Apparently at some point during the evening I had confessed to Posey my secret passion of wanting to do a short story collection instead of a novel for my thesis project along with my plans for a boozily plotted kidnapping scheme. Wait, had I just ruined the plan before I even knew what it was?

"What other thing?" Farmington asked.

"Nothing," Posey said. "Like he said, he was drunk."

"Yes, Drunk," I said. "Drunk..."

"If we're going to work together," Farmington said to me. "You're going to have to increase your verbal skills."

"Oh. Yeah. Sure. Wait. Really? You want to work with me on this."

"Make that your verbal and your listening skills."

Farmington kissed Posey on his way out of the house and I sighed deeply and then Posey smacked the back of my head.

"What the fuck?" She said.

My head grazed the coffee cup in front of her, sending it rolling off the table and crashing to the floor, which added an extra layer of ringing in my head.

"You could have blown everything."

"I wake up and the first thing I see is him standing over me with a water bottle?" I said. "Excuse me for being a bit off."

"I was trying to help you and you almost got both of

us —"

"Why are you helping me?"

"Do we really need to go through this again?"

"Again?"

"Last night. We had a long discussion about your goals and dreams. You cried a lot and threw up a bit. That's when you told me about the story collection and how you hate writing books with plots and want to write little stories of character."

"That sounds like something I would say..."

"And it sounds great. Great for you, because it's just the sort of thing Parker likes and good for him because, between you and me, his career's kind of in neutral and he could use an exciting book like this to generate some buzz for both of you."

"So you're out to help him, not me?"

"I've got to get to class, but —"

"Class isn't in session is it? I thought we were done with classes. I hope I haven't —"

"It's one of those two week mini semesters. Part of it meets here and then part of it meets up at a ski lodge in Traverse City. Parker's coming with me, so you two should get as much done as you can in the next day or so to set the foundation. Come back over here around five and I'll make dinner for all of us and some wine and you two can work while I pack."

They both then left me alone on the couch to deal

with what had just happened. I was happy, until I started thinking more about it. Thinking has always been a weak point of mine. While my own hyper-self-awareness gave me my strength as a writer, it was a double-edged sword that routinely led to paralyzing panic. In this case it led to more vomiting. And then a shower.

· · ·

I WAS at a table in the university library writing when Parker Farmington found me. Rather, I was doing what passed for writing in my special world. After typing a few words in the open document on my computer, I switched over to Twitter and tried to build my brand. It was a nice place for a socially backward guy who was good with words to build connections in the crime fiction community without creeping anyone out. I managed to ride the line between clever and offensive for a while before typing something stupid and deleting it. Then I typed a few more words before Googling recent book deals. I was always hoping to see a rash of books sort of like the one I was working on but not too similar so I wouldn't be accused of piggybacking. I padded my total word count for the day with an inane dialogue sequence I was sure would later be deleted and was about to shut down my laptop when Farmington sat down across from me.

"The only reason I agreed to your inane little plan," Farmington said, "is because I need Posey to keep her mouth shut about our relationship."

"Because sleeping with your teaching assistant is creepy and against the rules even if you're the same age?"

I thought about that for a second after I said it. We were all the same age, but Posey and I were stuck in neutral and stuck in Detroit while Parker was a prodigy just passing through.

"Because I've got something going that I don't want stymied. She needs to think you and I are really working on this new project of yours."

"Even though we won't be."

"But if you tell her we are and act like we are, I'll try to get you an extension and maybe we'll get your thesis signed and get you out of here next year."

"If you would have signed my thesis form the first time around, I wouldn't—"

"If I signed off on that literary swill we'd both be ruined."

"What am I supposed to do for a whole goddam year? I have a fellowship in New York with money and a teaching job now."

"Shhhhh. We're in a library. I can maybe get you something in the writing center to hold you."

"Maybe? *Maybe?* No maybe. Sign my fucking thesis or I'll go to the Dean about you and Posey."

"I'm a man of letters, a man of taste, a man of education," Farmington said in a pompous voice as though he were addressing a jury. "How many times have you been on academic probation again?"

I knew he was right. While I'd been able to overcome the bulk of my personality issues that resulted in my spectacular flameout from a top-tier writing program, I still wasn't a very good student and spent more time writing and reading what I wanted instead of what was assigned. But even if I couldn't tell the Dean about Farmington's relationship and get him fired, there was one other person I could tell. While complaining about how badly she wanted to have sex in Parker Farmington's house and comforting me on my plummeting career prospects, Posey Wade also talked about her psychotic bounty hunter brother and how much he hated the men she was involved with.

If I could get Posey's brother in the same room with Farmington, maybe we could strong arm Farmington into signing the thesis approval form.

"You're smiling," Farmington said. "It's kind of creepy. Are you on board?"

"Yeah. Yes. Yes. I'm on board."

CHAPTER 3

My plan seemed simple enough: harness the rage of Posey Wade's crazy bounty hunter brother to scare Farmington into signing my thesis approval form. But the more I thought about it, the more opportunity I saw to add insult to injury. I was also going to teach Farmington a lesson.

I envisioned dragging Farmington around to the nastiest parts of Detroit to show him the impact of crime on society. It would open his eyes beyond the little suburban realism stories he was so fond of. And a bounty hunter would give me the courage to visit some of the places I'd written about — or wanted to write about — but never felt safe enough to visit alone.

A quick Google search gave me an address for Wade Bail and Recovery in downtown Detroit across from the courthouse. It only took fifteen minutes to get down to the office, but after parking in a fenced off lot a couple blocks down the street, I sat in the car for another 30 minutes contemplating what I was about to do. It didn't take long for it all to overwhelm me again, but instead of leaving, I pushed it to the back of my brain, dug into my storehouse of petty resentment, and loaded up on Hostess orange cupcakes and Red Bull.

Titus Wade's office was unlocked and I entered feeling confident and lightheaded from the sugar rush. A door off to the side swung open and a hulking bald man stomped out, holding a bloody shirt to his forearm.

"Who are you?"

"Are you Titus Wade?"

"Get out of here," the man said.

"If we could just talk for a minute, I'm kind of in a bad place and need help."

Wade ignored me and went back out through the side door. I followed. It wasn't a bathroom as I'd expected, rather a storage room with three safes and two file cabinets. There was a closed door I figured was a maintenance closet or link to another office, and an open door that led outside where I found Wade wiping down the inside of a large black pickup truck. My confidence in my plan was rapidly fading.

"I'm in a workshop with your sister; I'm a writer, and the professor hates me."

Wade stopped wiping the truck and looked at me. I knew he hated Farmington as much as I did but I didn't want to set him off yet.

"I need somebody to show him the nasty places in the city, scare him a little, but—"

"I find people, I chase people, and occasionally I shoot people—"

"Oh God, don't shoot him."

"If he owes you money, I can get it out of him for you," Wade said. "If all you want me to do is drive him around town, then get yourself a goddam cab."

I hung my shoulders in defeat, but didn't move from my spot in front of Wade's truck. I wasn't selling my plan well enough. This is why I was a writer. I was never very good with words in person, but I could make them dance on the page. I could find just the right rhythm and combination and word choice to make even the most complicated idea or situation seem manageable. But Titus Wade didn't seem like the sort of fellow who would read a note explaining why he should join me on a quest to capture his sister's fornication partner. So I went with the skill of last resort: unfiltered rage.

"This guy is fucking your sister," I said, "and he's fucking with my career. We need to take him down."

There was enough of a pause in Wade's movement that I thought maybe I got to him. But the shields came almost immediately back up and he gave me the brush.

"Sorry," Wade said. "Call me if you ever need bail."

• • •

I LEFT Wade's office flipping between anger and depression.

I'd swear and punch things, then cry a little and wonder if I'd be able to find anything interesting to write about while working as a fast food clerk. My pain threshold eventually exceeded my anger and I stopped punching things, but I couldn't shake the depression. I'd spent the entire year focused only on getting my thesis finished and approved for the fellowship to New York. So much so that I neglected almost everything else in my life.

I let my car payments slide (I wouldn't need a car in New York City), hadn't paid rent in more than six months, (housing is included as part of the fellowship), allowed my cell phone to be disconnected (the only people who called were collection agents and my mother) and I'd neglected every personal and professional relationship once my letters of recommendations had been secured. The only person I had been more interested in than myself over the past year was Parker Farmington.

I tolerated his jokes, snide comments, the inane revision requests; I'd vaulted through every petty hoop Farmington had thrown in my path, all to please the only person who could stand in the way of my dream. Some of it had actually made my manuscript better, and early on we shared some nice conversations about our favorite crime writers, but as the year wore on and I talked more about New York, Farmington increased his intimidation and foolishness. It wasn't much of a reach to suspect Farmington didn't want my success interfering with his.

Now *I* was stuck in neutral in Detroit and couldn't find any way to accept that. I tried rational discussion with Farmington, which neither of us seemed to have any skill for, and I was becoming increasingly convinced I would have to get Farmington's signature onto that paper by force. Alone, it was an impossible task.

But Posey could be the key. If I could convince her that it was in Farmington's best interest to sign off on my thesis she'd be the perfect partner. We'd talked enough about how torn she was between being a poet and following in her brother's footsteps as a bounty hunter that I knew she had the skills and gravitas I lacked. I went back to her house but she wasn't there, so I went to a McDonald's near campus that had free Wi-Fi.

Since I'd stopped paying rent, my landlord had become aggressive about hunting me down. He was an old Italian guy whose office was right next to the only entrance to the building and he was always there watching '80s action movies on VHS. He particularly favored the work of Sylvester Stallone and I'd been able to negotiate a pretty sweet deal on my rent by giving him my copy of *Over the Top*, in which Stallone plays a truck driver turned competitive arm wrestler; that was the missing piece in his collection. A few weeks ago, in what I assume was an attempt to rebuild our connection, he mentioned he was heading to Philadelphia for a Rocky tour. I took advantage of his absence, loading everything I could into my car and never looking back.

I spent most of my time in the university literary magazine office using their showers and comfortable couches to survive. My erratic hours and routine sleepovers made me look like a dedicated editorial professional rather than a landlord-dodging hobo. But after my encounter earlier on campus with Farmington I wasn't in any mood to risk a repeat confrontation, hence the trip to McDonald's to email Posey. She was always checking her email on her phone and this was something that didn't seem well-suited to a text message. I waited several minutes without a reply before the employees began giving me looks that suggested I either order something or go on my way. I was leaving when Posey snuck up behind me.

"Coffee," she said "Black. Then let's talk about your idea."

CHAPTER

4

I told Posey what I'd been up to during the first part of the day, from my conversation with Farmington at the library to my failed meeting with Titus. I told her I felt I had no other option than to kidnap Farmington and force him to sign the thesis approval form. When I was done, Posey kept her eyes focused on me without saying anything for several beats.

"My brother saw us once, you know, during…"

"I'm surprised Titus didn't kill him," I said.

"I don't know. Just…after what you were talking about, with your plan—"

"A very poorly designed and barely executed plan."

"You and I, we don't have anything. So maybe you can just be a regular guy. Like a friend. And my brother can see I can be with a guy and not, you know—"

"Fuck him?"

"It's exhausting. Every guy. Every teacher, every fucking

person I make contact with I've got to worry about what Titus will think. I've got to plan ahead and plot and scheme. It's just getting to be too much."

I nodded in agreement and wondered if I had enough change in my pocket to get a McChicken sandwich.

"But this can be the end of it," she continued. "And it can help all of us: you, me, even Parker. I've been floating for so long, and now, maybe with a little kidnapping and some life-changing discussions we can both anchor him down in our futures."

I really didn't want to think of a future with Farmington in it. And despite a few heartfelt moments, I still didn't trust Posey or her motives and could only see disaster for both of us. But what other choice did I have? My academic career was on the verge of collapse and I was not cut out for professional office life. I'd been locked once before into a boring job with a pregnant fiancée, thinking I'd lost my chance to chase my dream before a miscarriage and a rotten economy set me free. I wasn't going to waste this second chance.

So I slugged the rest of my coffee back, held out my hand for Posey and said, "I can't even attempt a kidnapping without getting disoriented and tired, but if you help me we might be able to—"

"There's this guy I want you to meet," she said. "His name is Rickard. He's a security guard at the school and has helped me out a few times with Titus and shares your distaste for Parker. Kind of creepy and intense, but he has access to places we might need in the future. He's good with weapons and stuff and…well, he's kind of sweet."

I nodded and mentally planned my victory celebration.

"I just texted him," she said. "But it's probably best if I'm not here when you talk to him. He's…he's easily…he's skittish around me."

"Whatever," I said.

Twenty minutes after Posey left, Rickard still hadn't shown up so I figured I'd been had and left. I stopped at the bathroom on the way out and that's the last thing I remembered before blacking out.

CHAPTER

5

I woke up with my hands taped together and a ball gag in my mouth. The bench I was on was moving and for a brief second I thought I was still at McDonald's and my head was spinning. When I sat up I saw I was in the backseat of my own car with another man driving. My brain immediately went to bad places and I assumed I was on the sodomy express as punishment for my strip club antics. When the driver turned to face me after noticing I was awake, he slammed on the brakes. He reached back and pulled a snap near the side of my face and the ball gag fell loose.

"Fuck, man," he said. "I've never seen anybody knocked out so easily."

"I wasn't drugged?"

"You were barely hit. I got a little carried away and kinda misunderstood what Posey was thinking. Fucking AutoCorrect, right?"

"Huh," I muttered.

"Thought you might be on drugs or something. Maybe a heart condition. Never seen anybody go down like—"

"I get it. I'm a fucking bobble head. Whatever. You're Rickard, right? Why are you driving my car?"

"Got a body in mine."

I waited for him to laugh it off. He didn't. Maybe sodomy was a best-case scenario.

"Nobody recognizes yours," he continued. "Decent gas mileage too."

"Where are we going? And can you cut this tape off my hands?"

Rickard pulled the car off to the side of the road and I looked out the window to see where we were. It was one of the more nondescript sections of highway I'd seen in the city, so I assumed we were still close to downtown and, as such, I hadn't been out for long. Rickard opened the passenger door opposite me and threw me a small pocketknife.

"You can get in the front seat if you want," he said. "Your car and all."

As we passed each other I noticed he had a thin mustache and was wearing all black: a thick fisherman's sweater and a large stocking cap. Instead of a security guard, he looked like a cartoon burglar or a hipster dock worker.

He got back into the driver's seat and waited for my decision. I flipped open the knife and noticed it was sticky along the edge. Red and sticky. Maybe it was jelly. He could be the sort to butter and jelly his toast with a pocketknife. I cut my hands free and got into the front passenger's seat. I thought about running, but he didn't seem threatening really. Creepy, but not threatening.

I handed him his knife back and said, "Sticky."

"Told you I had a body in my car," he said.

So that was it then. The only question remained was whether I was going to be a victim or accomplice. When my seat belt was snapped and my door shut, Rickard pulled my car back onto the freeway and drove south I think. We were into Ohio before I began really wondering where we were going.

"Am I going to need to put plastic in my trunk?" I asked.

He ignored me so I went back inside my head to figure out where I was mentally, physically, and emotionally. I wasn't able to get a very good bead on the other two, but a few short minutes later, physically, I was in the parking lot of a storage facility that looked like it had been attacked by a gang with baseball bats and spray paint and then abandoned.

"Here," Rickard said, "is where shit gets interesting."

I couldn't help but note that could easily mean the physical location of the storage facility, and the current point in the narration that was my life. I just had to hope his definition of interesting was on the same page as my definition of interesting.

The only storage facility I'd ever visited at that point in my life was one of those sterile, over-lit, aluminum frame

places with a vaguely nautical theme that existed to house
the excess furniture of wealthy couples, degenerate spouses
between marriages, wealthy college students on their third
colleges, and the occasional homeless person from a well-to-
do but emotionally bankrupt family.

This storage facility seemed to exist only as a modular
and easy to clean meth lab complex. Instead of long rows of
storage cabinets like I'd seen in other facilities on television
and from the expressway, this facility was a weedy concrete
garden sprouting small metal sheds in even intervals. The
entire complex was fenced off with razor wire and that
seemed to be the sturdiest structure in the area. Rickard
drove my car around to the back parking lot where we had
a good view down the rows of sheds to the entrance gate
and cut the engine. Outside the temperature was on its way
down as the sun ended its brief appearance, replaced by the
dark, rolling gray clouds that are the trademark of Detroit
winters.

"This is your hideout?" I asked.

"In one of these lockers is a suitcase containing exactly
25 uncirculated packs of 100 two dollar bills that represent
payment from a publisher for a book Parker Farmington
wrote, with me, based on my life."

"Why would anybody care about the life of a security
guard?" I asked, regretting it immediately.

"Security guard is but one of many faces my true identity
takes. More will be revealed as we grow together on our

journeys."

My WTF meter was off the charts but I suspected my own quirks were enough to creep out others so I gave him the benefit of the doubt temporarily.

"So we're stealing the money?"

"You want Farmington, fine, I'll help you snag the twee little buffoon, but the bills are mine."

"Twenty-five hundred bucks seems a bit skimpy to be getting so worked up over."

"The publisher is an odd fellow, loves the number 2, loves $2 bills, but doesn't care anything about numismatics."

"So he pays in cash? Whatever, right?"

"If we're to be paired, our focus must be in sync."

"I'm focused. I'm ready."

"A man who cares more about the denomination of a bill than the bill itself is a fool. Are you a fool?"

I wasn't in any mood for mind games and I kept watching Rickard, wondering how he was connected to this and why he'd be helping Parker with anything, but I was out of good options and this seemed the least awful of my bad options.

"The bills are worth more than $2500," I said.

Rickard smiled a wide beaming smile and looked down at a plastic children's watch with the Detroit Tigers logo on it and said, "We go in ten minutes."

"How much are they worth?"

"Forty dollars," he said.

"Jesus Christ," I said. "You're a loon." You'd rather have

$40 in cash rather than $2500 just because it doesn't match the denomination? I love quirks but this is too much. I'm done. Jesus."

I took seven steps and turned around to give one more last zinger when he said:

"Each."

Oh.

I did the math in my head and came up with $100,000. Not a fortune, but enough to make a difference.

"I'm supposed to give Parker a vial of my blood," he said, tapping his wrist and holding it up for me to see.

"Blood?"

"For the book."

"You talk about my focus and what I need to be doing, but you gotta stop talking in riddles, man. My brain is fried. I'm an emotional grenade and I just candle handle this shit.

"The publisher specializes in rare production techniques to make boring books special. In this case, he's adding a vial of my blood to the printing ink for the book. It's not as creepy as you'd think and is quite common in comic books. Shit. Duck down. He's here."

I should have been worrying about the mental state of the guy I was hitching my future to, but for some reason the only thought running through my mind was that I still couldn't believe that a pretentious hack like Parker Farmington had a book deal.

CHAPTER 6

Rickard handed me the sticky knife again.

"In case," he said.

He reached in front of me into the glove box and took out a small revolver that looked like it had been pulled from a swamp. It was faded and crusted with gunk and looked like the only danger it posed was tetanus.

"What's the plan?" I asked.

"We'll go down there, do what I'm supposed to do and wait for a good time to hit him."

There was a gusty wind whipping around outside, making it even colder than it looked. I had on a wool pea coat I'd purchased at a military surplus store and for once, my choice to look artsy paid practical dividends. I was still wearing the red Flash t-shirt I'd worn to the department party and over that I had a hooded gray Detroit State University sweatshirt.

The coat blocked the wind and kept my hands (and the accompanying knife) warm, while the hood helped cover my head and face for warmth and concealment purposes. My outfit helped slim my portly writer figure and his thick sweater and thick hat bulked up his rather scrawny build, giving us both the impression of muscle to be thrown around.

As we approached the storage locker, Titus Wade pulled up in his truck while Farmington was unlocking the door. At first nothing seemed amiss and Parker didn't run away when he turned and saw Wade coming his way. Rickard stopped and motioned for me to do the same.

Their discussion quickly escalated to a physical confrontation with Farmington swatting at Wade. For a brief second I laughed at his pathetic attempts at self-defense, but then Wade reached around to his back and pulled out a small black box he shoved into Farmington's neck. I'd seen enough news reports recently on police brutality to recognize a Taser. Rickard and I rushed toward the locker. Wade had Farmington in the back seat of his truck and was slamming it shut when we caught up to them and yelled for him to stop. Wade made a brief move like he wanted to go back to the storage shed before leaving, but quickly reconsidered and jumped in his truck and sped away.

I started to run back to my car to follow them, but Rickard kept moving further toward the storage shed. Wade must have thought about going back for the money, but when we showed up he cut his losses and ran. I didn't want to think about the sort of plan he had where Farmington was more important to him than a bag of money.

"Let's go," I yelled.

Rickard kept walking toward the shed.

"I'm getting my money."

"But we can't let Wade—"

"Do what? So he stays with Wade instead of you for a little bit. This way we get the money and the professor."

My emotions were swirling in the same cocktail of panic they had the night of the department party, so I took a breath and calmed myself. I could dredge up enough bad thoughts to keep me pushing through the ugliness of a kidnapping, but a scam with cash and Wade holding the professor only spelled doom.

And yet I kept dwelling on the things I could do with that money. I led a life with minimal expense and minimal commitment to maximize my chances of surviving on my future writing income, making even a small infusion of instant cash go a long way. All I wanted was Farmington's signature on my thesis approval form. With the money though, I wouldn't need it."

"Come on," Rickard said through my brain farts. "He might come back."

I sprinted back to Rickard as he was fiddling with the lock on the storage shed. The lock was an electronic keypad on a black iron box. While it was one of the more complex pieces of engineering I'd seen to date, I was surprised at the ease with which Rickard was typing in a combination and opening the lock.

"You know the combination?"

"Baseball," he said. "You wouldn't understand."

He had the lock open, but was having trouble getting it off of the door to open it.

"I know baseball," I said. "Pitchers, catchers, Ball Park hot dogs and overpriced beer. How does that—"

Rickard snapped his head around and glared at me.

"You don't *know* baseball," he said. "You don't know the soul of the game or the way it gets into your brain and just…"

He left it at that and I wasn't stupid enough to chase him into whatever crazy place he'd pulled that from. So I stuck my little girly hand in the space between the lock and the door and helped him tug it open.

"Aside from the rusty doors and CIA surplus locks, this doesn't seem like a very secure place to stash a bag full of cash," I said. "You could probably take out one of these side panels with a screwdriver and a strong breeze, bypassing the lock completely."

Inside the shed, Rickard bumped around a bit while I stayed closer to the door, trying to get a peek of what else was in the shed. There didn't seem to be much else, but I saw a couple of cardboard boxes in the middle of the floor. Before I could contemplate the boxes, their contents, or my uncomfortably burgeoning curiosity in Parker Farmington's life and secrets any further, Rickard pushed by me with a large suitcase in one hand and a small handgun in the other.

"How old is that thing?" I asked, following him back to my car.

"Newish. Fired I'm sure, but untraceable."

"The suitcase," I said. "It's in great condition, but good god, it's got to be older than me. How much do you think something like that would go for on eBay?"

He didn't answer me, we made it to the car without any further trouble, and as I settled into my seat I began to imagine something better for myself. I imagined my share of the money going into a bank account with low interest and high security. I've never been good with my real life money, but in my fantasies I turn into Mr. Fiscal Security. But all it took was one bad turn of the key and I knew there wasn't going to be anything good for me coming out of this. Rickard tried to start my car a couple more times before finally looking to me.

"Fucking American cars," he said, getting out of the car.

I didn't want to leave the car so I rolled down my window to yell at him.

"Where are you going?"

"Unless you've got a backup, we need to get my car."

"With the body?"

"I know someone who can help us with that. She's paralyzed, and a bit of a bitch, but last resorts and all of that, right?"

I nodded and wondered if it came down to it, whether I'd prefer jail or death.

CHAPTER 7

Rickard was back in the car with me when a rusty blue full-sized van pulled up next to us. I tried to move my hand to check my door lock, but my arm was numb from the cold and wouldn't move.

"Check the locks," I said. "Make sure they're—"

"That's the Cavalry, man. Rescue bitch is here."

Rickard moved from the car to the front seat of the van in the time I was able to pump enough energy into my arms and legs to get my own door open. I stood without closing the door for several seconds, wondering what to do with my car. Rickard rolled his window down and stuck his head out of the van.

"Want me to come back for you, leave you alone to mourn your golf cart?"

"I think I still have Triple A," I said. "They made me pay a huge lump sum when I tried to cancel and I wonder if I should call them."

"We got a ride," Rickard said.

He popped his head back inside the van and came back out with a joint hanging off his lips and a beer can in his hand.

"A ride with beverage service."

"You think maybe it's just the weather? I mean, you think we could—"

"Your ride is shit, man. Leave it and maybe somebody strips it, you get the insurance and get something new with a real engine."

I didn't really care much about the car. In New York I wouldn't need it and if I stayed in Detroit I wouldn't be able to afford it. But I still hesitated to Rickard's growing irritation. It wasn't my car that concerned me; it was the car waiting for us with the body in the trunk, and more immediately, this rescue ride. Giving up my car was giving up control of the situation which didn't let me off the hook if it all went south, and put me at the mercy of a man with more in mind for Parker Farmington than a forced signature and cash swipe.

Rickard tossed the suitcase on the seat next to me when I got in the van.

"Out of curiosity," I said. "How much is in here?"

Rickard leaned over his seat and twisted back to face me.

"Jesus, a little discretion," he said.

I pointed to the old woman driving who had a pair of headphones on, blocking out our conversation.

"She's not even listening."

"Those are for looks, she knows exactly what's going on."

"Huh," I said. "Sorry."

"You're a writer, but maybe can you do some math too?"

"You want me to count it?" I asked.

"Jesus," he said again, pointing himself toward front again. "Maybe I need some fucking headphones."

The ride was silent after that. The old woman never said anything, I never learned her name, and twenty minutes later we were pulling around to the back entrance of the Saddle Ranch where a clean, but older model Buick the size of a small barge was waiting for us.

Rickard must have noticed me evaluating the size of his car, because he said, "Believe it or not, this is smaller than my last one."

"I had one like this in high school and right into college," I said. "The air didn't work and the back floorboards were rotted out, but it warmed up nice in the winter and got surprisingly good gas mileage for an old boat."

Rickard went to the trunk and popped it open. I looked over my shoulder and noticed the van and hobo lady hadn't left yet.

Rickard said. "We can probably fit the professor in here next to Steve."

"Steve?"

"My trunk buddy here. I had a little trouble with —"

"I don't need to know anything about Steve. I don't even

want to know that his name is Steve."

"You gonna keep yammering like that, do it while you help me lift."

I absentmindedly grabbed Steve's feet—dammit, the name was stuck in my head now—and stutter-stepped backward away from Rickard's giant Buick. He swung Steve...er, the body's top half around and took the lead, walking us back toward the hobo van.

Wait a minute.

"Why are we taking him to her?" I asked.

"The kind lady in the van has offered to help us with the disposal situation so that we can—"

"Wait. What?" I asked.

"She's gonna take the suitcase and the body so we can—"

I dropped my end of Steve and stopped walking.

"What kind of moron are you?"

Rickard dropped his end too and put his hands on his hips.

"You're not exactly a fount of alternative ideas," he said.

I dragged Steve by his legs back to the Buick and tried to shove him back into the trunk. It took me several tries, with Rickard watching and not offering to help, but I finally got him in. I tossed the suitcase in after the body and slammed it shut.

"Keys," I said.

I crawled into the driver's seat and waited patiently for Rickard to bring me the keys, but he didn't. I looked out the back window and didn't see him behind the car and I wondered if he left the keys in the van. Rickard appeared next to me in blur and opened the driver's side door again.

"You could have just put the keys in—"

Rickard smacked me in the side of the head and grabbed the collar of my shirt. The smack stung more than it hurt. He tugged at my collar and I rolled out of the car to avoid being strangled by my own shirt. My hope that it was an isolated instance of his "unbalanced" behavior was dashed by a kick to my stomach. I prepped for another to follow, but there wasn't one. Instead, Rickard rolled me over and stuck the sticky red knife to my throat. I looked in his eyes for some sign that his demon wire had been tripped, but his eyes were calm, his facial movements steady.

"Steve goes in the van," he said.

He didn't elaborate. The knife dug deeper into my skin, though Rickard didn't seem to be applying any extra pressure. The calm attitude, skill with weapons, and hair trigger would have all been very intriguing from a character standpoint if I hadn't been the one under the knife. When the knife finally pierced my skin Rickard pulled it away. I half expected him to lick the knife or sniff it or something, but he was not going to fall into standard villain clichés. At that point I wasn't sure there was a hero in my story, just varying degrees of villain.

Rickard removed himself and his knife from my personal space and once again I found myself holding the feet of a corpse, trying to load it into a handicap accessible van.

"Try around the back," the lady said.

I was kind of shocked when she spoke. I'd assumed she was a mute as well as handicapped. I'm sure that doesn't say much for my sensitivity toward the handicapped, but hey, at least I'm aware of my prejudices, right?

"Van can take a fucking wheelchair," Rickard mumbled, "but no good way to load a folded up body."

He tossed me the keys and I stared at them like one of those pocket puzzles they give you at truck stop restaurants to distract you from the poor service and depressing atmosphere. I gripped them tightly and pondered their irony. They represented freedom from this mess, from the consequences of my arrogance and poor planning, and more importantly from the immediate vicinity of Rickard and the mystery van. But Rickard was already in the passenger seat so I couldn't steal the car from him and if I tried to run from him I suspected the crippled hobo lady would run me over.

So I continued staring at the keys until Rickard, once again, leaned out a window and hollered at me.

"Let's go," he said. "We need to see what we're fighting for before this snow gets too bad."

CHAPTER 8

"These guys," Rickard said, smacking the radio in the Buick. "Moron hosts and moron callers dissect everything about baseball but what's important."

He was listening to a sports talk radio station I listened to myself when I got sick of the forced banter and homogenous rotation of the same 10 songs of your chosen genre that was the state of modern radio. I'd heard Detroit had a vibrant music scene but I'd never had the patience or desire to dig for it so I was stuck with the same songs you could hear in Scottsdale or Schaumburg or Sherman Oaks or any other bland suburb.

"Nice radio," I said, running my finger along the screen of a shiny chrome box that looked more expensive than the car itself.

"Satellite," he said. "I'm kinda obsessed with baseball and this lets me listen in all over the country and see what they're saying about our boys."

"The Tigers?"

"Look at these empty streets," Rickard said.

I vaguely recognized the area. We were on the immediate outskirts of the downtown area but I couldn't place exactly where until Rickard continued talking about baseball and I realized we were near the old spot of Tiger Stadium. To hear old guys talk about it, you'd think the neighborhood was some kind of magical baseball heaven. But in actuality, it was just as run down as the rest of the city, if slightly more populated due to the higher concentration of white people left over from its days as the Irish neighborhood known as Corktown.

What was left of the stadium was a corner chunk of faded gray steel that had been the corner of the stadium behind home plate. The field was still there, lovingly maintained by a small group of fans, but the fields surrounding it were weedy and littered with trash.

"This place is like a fucking graveyard now, but back in '84, there were crowds and cars and miniature bats being handed out."

I nodded along, wondering if this was the speech he gave Steve before doing whatever he did to get him into the trunk.

"You were here back then?"

"First time my dad took me to a game in years. Money was tight, he was always getting laid off and that free little wooden bat was my only souvenir."

He didn't say anything else for several minutes while he circled the block, slowing every so often as a young black guy in a security guard uniform walked the outline of the weedy lot. Finally, Rickard circled one last time to the back side of the lot.

"I could list all of the stats, the player bios, all of the box score shit, but what sticks in my head are my memories of the stadium: the smells, the sounds, and the voice of Hickey Ernest calling the plays."

He paused again, this time only briefly. Then said, "Fucking Hickey Ernest."

"When I was younger, seven or eight," I said, "before my dad turned into an asshole, we used to do work around the house and in the yard on the weekends. He always had baseball games on the radio with Hickey Ernest."

"The times we went to the stadium my pop would bring one of those little radios to plug in his ear so we could still get his commentary. Everything I know about baseball, Detroit, and being a man I learned from Hickey Ernest."

Said the man with a fresh body in the trunk and a bloody knife in his pocket.

"It sounds like maybe you don't care for the man anymore," I said.

"He changed. We all changed, but he changed worse. For the worse."

It seemed like he wanted to say more, but the security guard was moving swiftly in our direction.

"Sir," the guard said.

Rickard didn't say anything and neither of us moved. I looked down and saw Rickard's hand moving around in the pocket with the knife. He wouldn't really kill this guy in front of me. Would he? In broad daylight?

"Sir," the guard repeated. "I thought we had an agreement from this morning. You told Steve—"

"I don't see Steve around," Rickard said.

"Please leave."

"Come on," I said. "The longer Farmington is alone with Wade—"

"You ever go to a game, you know, when this place was real?"

Rickard was talking around me to the guard.

"Not here," the guard said after a second or two of contemplation. "But the new place, they did good with it and I've taken my kid a couple times."

Rickard nodded in slow agreement with his head down then looked up and surveyed the whole field. The last blast of cold weather through town had left a layer of frost over everything, giving the field the look of a ball diamond preserved under hockey ice.

"It's a different game now," Rickard continued. "Different people, different spirit. I just want to hold onto the good times a bit longer."

"They're really cracking down though on you people coming through here. I can't be taking my boy to no games if

I'm on the unemployment line, you know?"

"My friend here and I," Rickard said, nodding toward me, "we have a common acquaintance who could have saved this place."

They both looked at me. I had no idea what he was talking about.

"The Professor," Rickard said. "Wouldn't give me my share of *our* money in time to save the corner."

"Right. That's what they called it here. The Corner."

"No, the corner is behind home plate. The actual home plate, for that matter, that's now in Toledo."

The guard saw his last opportunity to get us out of there and mumbled something about us maybe heading to Toledo to try our luck. For some reason it worked this time and Rickard motioned for me to follow him back to the car.

"Make sure you get that son of yours to a real ball park before he's too old," Rickard said by way of goodbye. "Fenway or Wrigley. Some place with character."

• • •

"STEVE WAS a...I mean that body was a security guard?" I asked in the car, driving away from the ball field.

"You said you didn't want to know anything about it."

"No...you're right. Let's talk about what you said about Farmington and his deal with you and how you were going to save this corner. What did I get myself in the middle of?"

"Sons, fathers, legacies, back stabbing, misplaced trust.

It's like that guy Shakespeare: real dramatic and shit."

I'd never been a standout in any of my literature seminars, but I spent enough time in them that something was bound to seep into my subconscious. So as Rickard talked, I started having a mishmash of flashbacks to Native-American literature, Greek mythology, Roman mythology, biblical stories, and a screenwriting story seminar that I drove to Chicago for on the night after Melissa lost the baby.

"You're a trickster," I said. "You and Posey. Devious beings that exist to fool around in my world and manipulate events for your own entertainment."

"Hmmm," he said.

"But there's another character. I'm not the most important character."

"Me?"

"Farmington. I'm telling it, but he's my mirror character. The one I'm supposed to learn through."

Rickard stared dumbfounded at me and I didn't really blame him. It sounded ludicrous out loud but made perfect sense to me. It put my entire life in perspective. I was meant to tell great stories, but before I could do that I needed to develop as a storyteller through life experiences. The universe's first attempt had almost worked. Some of the most honest, disturbing, and brilliant writing I did was in the midst of my worst trials with Melissa. Then I squandered all of that honesty writing cheesy stories about hit men and strippers and self-congratulatory, navel gazing stories about writers.

"That look on your face," Rickard said. "It's like you're playing with the dolls in your head."

"Farmington was right. I was selling myself short with the stuff I was writing. It wasn't the crime part that sucked, it was the sucking part that sucked."

"Wow. Yeah. You're great with the words."

"I was almost married once," I said. "She was pregnant and I dropped out of school and gave up writing and took an office job in a cubicle and thought that was going to be the rest of my life. I even went out and bought a briefcase."

"Sucker."

"She lost the baby then left me and I got a second chance at the life I was meant to have. I don't ever want that other life. That is no life. I can't do that. And Farmington holds the key to saving me from that."

"Let's go get him then."

"First though, I'm hungry. I have low blood sugar and I feel myself starting to drag."

I'd lost track of the time and emerged from my thought bubble unsure of how much real time had passed. I was tweaked about my self-realizations and excited to jump into my vision quest, but when my blood sugar drops, I lose focus easier than normal and my decision-making skills completely disintegrate.

"How about Taco Bell?" I said. "There's one near here, isn't there?"

"By the college. I got a burrito there once at like 2am after I stabbed a guy at a bar."

I stared at him and knew my energy was already depleted because I didn't jump out of the car right then.

"He didn't die," Rickard said. "Not from that. He asked me to stab him. He had a vest on."

I nodded and thought about whether I wanted tacos or a burrito. Rickard tapped his fingers obnoxiously on the steering wheel navigating through the college area. Two blocks from the restaurant we noticed the police car following us. Rickard was the first to notice it was a campus police officer just before the cruiser rammed us from behind.

CHAPTER 9

Rickard put his knife on the dashboard and rummaged around in the glove box while we waited to see what the occupant of the police cruiser would do. I was expecting Rickard to pull a gun, so when he came out with a small pack of Elmo branded baby wipes I laughed out loud.

"It's a woman," Rickard said, still looking in the rear view mirror.

"Who, Elmo? His voice is actually done by a—"

"The cop. Behind us. Keep your hands in clear view."

He used two separate wipes to clean off his hands before passing the pack over to me and placing both of his hands on the steering wheel. I held the wipes without doing much but watching Rickard waiting to see what his next move would be. I wondered if the wipes were part of the routine of his kills.

I was still confused by Rickard's wipes as the officer made

her stumbling way toward his side of the car. After a second or two keeping his hands on the steering wheel in plain sight, Rickard went back into his pockets and pulled out the gooey blood knife and put in on the dashboard in front of him. I waited for him to ask me for one of the wipes to clean off his knife as he'd done with his hands, but he didn't.

Finally I said, "Does it always have to be Elmo wipes?"

He kept his eyes straight ahead, with the occasional detour to the rearview mirror to gauge the officer's approach.

"What?"

"The wipes," I said. "For your ritual. Do they always have to be Elmo wipes? And why don't you use them to clean your knife? I saw the blood on it earlier when I was cutting the fence. Why do you just clean your hands?"

"Ritual? What are you talking about?"

I held the wipes up and shook the pack.

"You were cleansing your hands I assume. But why only your hands? You don't strike me as the religious sort and I thought for a minute maybe you see your hands as weapons and want to keep them clean, but in that case why would you keep your knife dirty. Unless…"

"They were on sale at Target. I bought them yesterday because I knew I'd be going into some nasty places."

"So you let the knife take the brunt of the nastiness," I said. "Now I get it. Sort of like a sin eater."

"Jesus Christ."

"The knife is the tool but you can clean your hands before

each kill to keep your soul clean."

I put the wipes back in the glove box and leaned back in my seat to bask in the glow of my superior profiling skills.

"I want a shower after being at that storage facility," Rickard said. "I've been there before and I always want a shower after I'm around Titus Fucking Wade. But this is Michigan in the middle of winter and I've got shit to do. Even if I had the time to shower after every fucking encounter I don't like, my skin couldn't handle it. I'd dry out like a fucking sponge. So I bought the Elmo wipes. Not only were they on sale, they have aloe in them. It turns out I like the aloe; it keeps my skin from splitting open. So keep your bullshit Dateline special theories inside your fucking head or I'll rip your tongue out and wrap it in one of those wipes to keep it from bleeding on my upholstery. And Jesus Christ how long is it going to take that woman to get to my window?"

"I think she's drunk," I said.

He'd been spouting nothing but clipped phrases and half-baked sentence fragments since we'd paired up. To see him rant made me smile. He wasn't the first person to crack under the pressure of my slow-burning personality quirks, but he was certainly the scariest. As I wallowed in my pleasant sense of success, Rickard lost patience waiting for the cop and hopped out of the car to meet her.

I glanced up at the rearview mirror to get a better view of the unfolding catastrophe and I watched in amazement and horror as the cop sobered up suddenly and turned into an action hero. She quickly diffused Rickard's surprisingly competent attacks and waved a Taser around briefly before snapping her hand out once at neck level, dropping Rickard.

I returned my attention to the car and my options for escape. My mind had only made it as far as wondering how many Elmo wipes I'd have to swallow to kill myself when I heard my window glass crack and then felt my head swell up with warm fuzzies.

• • •

WHEN I woke up again, I was in the backseat of Rickard's car and he was unconscious next to me. The officer was in the driver's seat looking at me in the rearview mirror.

"He's going to wake up soon," she said. "I need you to do me a favor."

"Huh?"

She handed me a business card with the Detroit State University Police Department logo in the corner and her name in a bland font across the middle: Sgt. Lindsey Buckingham, Campus Security Liaison.

"Like the guitar player?" I asked.

"Yeah. I got sick of all the fame and money and decided I'd rather spend my best years issuing DUIs to college students and investigating video game thefts."

"Do I know you?"

"That's his apartment there in front of you," Lindsey said. "You'll want to be inside when he wakes up. I gave him a stronger jolt because I wanted to talk to you first and it's not going to be pleasant for him when he wakes up."

She shifted in her seat and seemed to have trouble staying upright. I briefly thought the drunken stumbling bit was a setup so she could knock out Rickard, but now in close quarters I could see her sloshy demeanor was no act. She looked like a waterbed trying to stay propped against a wall.

After a few tries, she was able to find an angle where she could wedge her thick legs under the steering wheel enough to stop sliding to the floor. I stared at her legs and the slight roll of her stomach over her waist and found myself aroused for the first time in a while. It was an inappropriate reaction to a strange situation and I found I had to do my own bit of shifting to sit comfortably. She didn't seem to notice any of it.

Instead she said, "You know Titus Wade, right?"

"Oh," I said. "Shit."

My arousal dissipated as quickly as it set in.

She must have found out what I was planning and was here to punish me. That would explain why she was a campus officer as opposed to a city cop. I wondered if Posey was the one who turned me in. The question now was whether Buckingham was going to address the issue professionally or, if she was a friend of Wade's, help him get his kicks torturing me first.

"I need you to let me know when you find him," she said.

I looked down again at the card in my hand and, what should have been the reassuring police logo in the corner.

There didn't seem to be a shortage of reasons for a cop to want to find Titus Wade, but the number of reasons that involved me was more limited and most likely involved using me as a shield/bait/fall guy/patsy.

"You're a cop," I said. "What can I do that you can't?"

"Campus cop," she said. "I might as well be a—"

She paused when Rickard twitched next to me.

"We need to get him inside," she said, beginning the acrobatics needed to open her door.

I looked out my window and saw we were in the parking lot of the Viking motel. It was the sort of single story L-shaped motel that would be charming and nostalgic along Route 66, but at the corner of a Detroit freeway ramp and a dead end service drive, it was just depressing and creepy.

"Take me with you," I said. "Leave Rickard here and we can go do whatever you need to do together."

She put her hand on my knee and tried to quiet me but drooled all over herself instead.

"He can help you," she said. "If he wakes up in this car that's going to be difficult for you."

"You act like you know everything about me," I said, rolling out of the car after her. "Everybody I run into says they know what's best for me and I'm fucking sick of it."

"I'm a pathetic romantic," she said, stopping in front of me. "You should know something about that."

She pulled a rolled up stack of papers from her back pocket and threw it to the ground near me. Despite the clueless demeanor I may project, I knew what she threw, I knew where she got it, and I knew why she wanted to talk specifically to me.

"You're in love with Titus Wade," I said, picking up the sheaf of papers.

"I am now. At first it was just because he was my first after I was...well, you wrote the story dammit."

"Not about you."

I looked down at the story in my hand. It was one of the first stories I wrote for Parker's workshop and I wrote it for Posey to show her I was capable of emotion as well as violence and snappy dialogue. The story was about a slutty and crooked vice cop who is attacked and almost raped, but miraculously saved. In the emotional moments after her attack she makes a deal with God to turn away from promiscuity and find one man to spend the rest of her life with.

"We've been up and down, and then he finally cut me loose," she said. "He's not built for that kind of emotion."

"If you only get one guy for the rest of your life, why Titus Wade?" I asked.

"Cheap wine and a Die Hard marathon. It's like oysters and Spanish fly for me."

I crumpled the story in my hands and held it tightly, trying to absorb some of the raw energy I'd managed to get on the page.

Rickard was starting to stir more consistently and Lindsey was able to stand on her own, so our moment was almost over. She was motioning for me to help her drag him into one of the middle units so I grabbed his feet and followed along. Rickard was scrawny, but unconscious he was still more dead weight than a guy who spent more time at a computer and in his imagination than he did in a gym could handle. But Lindsey was doing all of the real work and I was doing little more than steering. The Tasering bothered me, but I wasn't particularly emotional over the fact I was carrying a body in a parking lot for the second time that day. I suppose that was its own indictment of my leaking morality.

We got Rickard inside and onto a rust-colored sofa that was comically low to ground. As Lindsey was leaving, a wiry black guy with giant yellow-tinted eyeballs and a narrow mouth with three overhanging teeth bounded out of the bathroom. He was dressed in a pristine white tank top and blue sweat pants two sizes two big that still had the crackle of new clothes about them. He looked briefly at all of us and then left without a word.

"These locks are shit," Lindsey said.

I looked around the room and wondered if I might be able to find something to eat while I waited for him to fully revive.

"I don't suppose you want to go to Taco Bell?" I asked Lindsey.

"Titus is cooking up something stupid with your professor. I'm in no shape to look for him and would fuck it up if I did find him on my own."

"So it's me and Rickard to the rescue," I said, pointing to Rickard.

"I love your story," she said. "It made me realize I'm not alone. Thank you."

"How did you get it anyway?"

"Titus's sister likes you quite a bit. She expects big things from you. Call me when you find him."

I stood at the door confused for several minutes after Lindsey left until my need for food and a toilet overcame my daydreaming. Rickard slept soundly while I snacked on cold pizza and generic Pop Tarts I'd managed to locate in the fridge. I thought about turning on the small television, but I couldn't stop staring at the shrine in the corner. It was mostly made up of Detroit Tigers bobble head dolls from the '80s to the 2006 World Series run, but there were some other character novelties, including two small stuffed finger puppets of the team's mascot, Paws. Two large orange candles and a handful of dollar store Mardi Gras beads in Tigers orange and blue, along with a framed portrait of Hickey Ernest completed the creepy alter. I flashed back to my conversation with Rickard back at the baseball field and his comments to the security guard there about Steve. The body in the trunk named Steve.

Rickard was starting to move and I suspected I only had a few more seconds to myself before he was fully back on the grid. And in those few minutes I made a snap decision and got the hell out of there. I jumped in Rickard's car and drove away from the hotel, trying to remember exactly where the Taco Bell was.

CHAPTER 10

My first instinct was to get out of Detroit. I thought about starting over somewhere new or maybe even moving to New York City on my own and writing without a fellowship. But I couldn't do it. I didn't just want to write, I wanted to be a writer and that meant a lifestyle that I'd gambled my immediate future on with Parker Farmington, who had failed me and put me in this mess in the first place. I wanted Parker Farmington to sign my thesis form so I could fulfill the second chance I'd been given. And I didn't want this day hanging over my head, always wondering if a cop was going to show up and charge me.

I'd wanted to be a writer since I was in elementary school, when I first started thinking about career options outside of astronaut and professional booger farmer. I was not shy about proclaiming my future career, and many well-meaning teachers and gift-stumped affiliated adults took to buying me books on writing. I read all of them and absorbed their fluffy messages and continued typing away at my awful short stories and novels that only made it to page twenty.

The first one that finally made an impression on me was a screenwriting book that my high school choir teacher bought me by accident. The book extoled the virtues of the three act structure for plotting, which I would later find out is common knowledge among most writers, but it blew the doors off of my brain and gave me the structure I needed to start completing novel length manuscripts. It also gave me a way to structure my own view of life. Without ridged structure in my life, I can easily devolve into chaotic indifference, and the same was true with what I was going through with Farmington.

I needed to find Parker Farmington to make everything right. If I was to believe Lindsey Buckingham's drunken ramblings, Farmington was still in the city with Titus Wade for whatever big was going down in the evening. Everything that had happened to that point in the day could be lumped together under the Act One heading. But now the stakes had been raised, subplots had been set in motion, and the first twist had been introduced with Lindsey Buckingham and her request.

Now I was supposed to respond to the new information and use it to further my goal. While I would still have to find Farmington on my own, not a simple task at all as evidenced by my current lack of success, once I did find him I'd have a whole new playbook with Lindsey in getting Farmington away from Titus Wade.

In the drive-thru lane at the Taco Bell, I made the most of the scraps of cash in my wallet with creative manipulation of the value menu and a coupon I'd found in the parking lot for a free burrito. I was briefly tempted to camp out in a corner booth at the restaurant and work through my action plan while I ate, but I knew Rickard would be on the move soon looking for his car and the last thing we'd talked about was Taco Bell.

I didn't know enough about Titus Wade or Parker Farmington to hazard a guess on where they might be hiding out until zero hour, but I did know enough about the woman who linked them together and headed back to Posey's house. I wasn't sure what I would say to Posey if she was there; my plan was mostly hinging on her not being home and on my being able to sneak in.

I didn't notice the police car following me until I saw a flash of lights in my rearview mirror about six blocks from Posey's house. As I looked in the mirror, waiting for my fate, I noticed a familiar dent in the front bumper of the cruiser. Had Lindsey Buckingham chosen her job over her quest for love and was going to arrest me? Waiting for her to stumble up to my window again, all I could think of was the many ways her presence in my life could screw me over.

Her walk didn't have any more stability to it than the first time, and in fact, she seemed even more slovenly and drunk.

Once again, I thought about driving away. I could be out of the state before she could get back to her car and initiate pursuit, but allies were at a premium and until she proved otherwise, I counted Lindsey as an ally. So I waited for her.

And waited.

And to show how easily my attention span can diminish in even the most stressful situations, I was still startled when she knocked on my window four minutes later. I'd let my mind delve into the complicated question of whether the Chilito was truly extinct from the Taco Bell menu and whether the MexiMelt was a suitable enough substitute.

"I have a surprise for you," she yelled when I rolled down the window.

Her breath didn't reek of booze, but there was enough in the air to make it clear what she'd been up to in the brief interlude between our meetings.

"Are you drunk?"

She shook her head like a little child.

"Pills," she said. "Mostly. Booze makes me too tired and sick. We've got shit to do."

"Are you even on duty?"

She patted around her chest pockets then dug around in her pants pockets briefly before handing me a Detroit State University Police business card. It was just like the one she'd handed me earlier, but this time I paid attention to more than just the logo. She was listed as Sgt. Lindsey Buckingham.

"I'm a Special Liaison," she said. "I know people who

know people who know stuff…and shit. You know?"

"What do you want from me? You said to call you when I found Titus and you said I'd need Rickard to help me, but you left him so incapacitated that he was certain to try and murder me when he woke up and then you left me in that creepy motel room. But I survived, and got out, and got on with what you asked me to do. Find Titus Wade. And then —"

She leaned into the car as far as she could and put her finger on my lips.

"Jesus. Christ," she said. "You talk a lot. How can people stand to be around you for any length of time?"

"Stories? Plural? You've read more than one?"

"Come on back to my car. We can talk about it."

"Please leave me alone or I'm going to report you to whoever is more special than you in your department."

"You do need him and I've got him for you."

"Need who? Jesus? Are you a missionary now too?"

"Rickard. I told you before, you're going to need him. You can't find Titus without him. But I've got him for you."

I looked back in my rearview mirror to see if I'd missed anyone else in the car the last time I looked. There was nobody else in the car.

"Uhhhhh…"

"Come on," she said. "We've got to get going."

"What about this car?"

"It's not yours. Leave it."

I thought about my own car sitting in a vacant lot near a creepy storage facility on the Ohio border. I didn't have any particular attachment to the car, in fact I hated most everything about it, but I didn't like the thought of anything of mine being left abandoned like that.

"I need to go back to my car," I said, opening my door to push Lindsey back.

I stood with the door open and told Lindsey about the storage facility and what I saw there with Rickard and what I thought we might find there.

"Rickard was so bent on following Titus and getting away from the site," I said. "We didn't go back and look around once he saw where the money was going."

She nodded her head in a way that could have been contemplative or a warning that she was passing out.

"The money. Yes," she said. "Get in my car."

"Which he doesn't have any more."

"The money is the easy part. Titus. He's the enigma."

I closed the door of Rickard's car but remained standing where I was, unsure about riding with Lindsey in her current condition. Without knowing where Posey was, I didn't have any other leads on Titus or Parker so I got into the cruiser and hoped it was strong enough to protect me in the event of a crash.

Lindsey put the car in gear and pulled back onto the street with more dexterity and awareness than I would have expected from someone in her condition. That observation mixed with the agility I'd seen her display in her first takedown of Rickard made me suspect she was more of a functioning addict rather than a sloppy random druggie. Either way, I still felt safer with her than I had with Rickard and I'll admit her saying she liked my story had something to do with that.

After we'd been driving for several blocks and I was satisfied Lindsey wasn't going to pass out on me I said, "I understand your business in the downtown area. It's sort of like your jurisdiction because it's close to campus though not exactly on campus. But we're leaving the city, damn near the state. How will—"

"You saw the card right? Special Liaison?" She said. "I can liaise wherever I damn well please. You know why?"

I shook my head no.

"Because I've got the best interest of a faculty member at heart," she said. "And sometimes that interest is best protected on the DL by someone with a little more flexibility in their position, if you know what I mean."

I tried very hard not to think too much about how she said that word or it would be an awkward ride to the storage facility for both of us. She did raise an interesting point, a point that put me much closer to the right side of the law than the sketchy side. I was helping an officer of the university locate an endangered faculty member. As one of Parker Farmington's students I was in a perfect situation to provide information and support to Sgt. Buckingham. No one needed to know I had a hand in the faculty members' current predicament or that, if my own best interest didn't require Farmington's safe return, I'd be more than happy to let him rot in the care of Titus Wade.

"Why didn't you want me following up with Posey's roommates? They seemed like good —"

"It was a shit idea and if your next move would have been that stupid I would have left you at Rickard's house and sent cops for you."

"I want to start this day over again," I said. "No. I guess I'd want to start yesterday morning over again. Although the whole thing really started the night before that at the department Christmas party."

As I told Lindsey this, I realized I was more culpable in my actions than I wanted to admit. It wasn't just one bad choice one time that I could go back and redo. My current situation was the result of several choices made over a period of time without regard to how they impacted each other. The only way to fix it would be through another series of choices that I didn't screw up.

I'd been waiting for that one big move that would let me wipe the slate clean and let me start over, but that wasn't coming. My future was in successfully navigating these small choices with little margin for error.

"Is Rickard meeting us somewhere?" I asked.

"He's already with us. Not gonna let him out of my sight again."

"If you're hallucinating maybe you should let me drive."

She snorted a laugh and cocked her head back.

"He's in the way back seat, buddy. Maybe his mayhem can be—"

"He's in the trunk?"

"Unless you wanna swap seats with him."

This could be my first small choice toward the right path.

"No. That's fine," I said. "He can stay back there."

Or not.

CHAPTER 11

My car was still where I left it and it still had all of its wheels, including the one with the flat tire. The snow from earlier had melted into slushy rain and the corresponding change in temperature was thumping my sinuses like a windup monkey with a grudge. Changing a tire was something I wanted to do even less than deal with a moody, lovesick cop on the down end of a buzz or a baseball obsessed nut job and possible serial killer.

"I should have called Triple A to meet us here," I said.

Lindsey pulled next to my car. I replayed my last visit to the site in my head to see if I could pull anything useful from the replay, but I was too distracted by thoughts of Rickard in the trunk.

"So when you came with him," she said jerking her thumb toward the trunk. "That was your first time here?"

"After we have a look around, why don't we take care of

Rickard?"

She turned toward me and scratched the side of her head.

"Hmmm," she said, rummaging around under her seat. "I keep telling you we're going to need him, but I'm intrigued by your initiative."

"I can't focus with him back there. He's a loose end and I don't have the attention span for loose ends."

She scratched the side of her head again. I wasn't sure if it was a tick, or the drugs, or if it was her thinking motion.

"This is aggressive," she said, moving from scrounging under the front of her seat to leaning over and scrounging under mine. "Which I guess I should have expected considering your other stories. That one you wrote about the donkeys in Mexico, Jesus. But the last time we talked you seemed like you were always waiting for something to happen instead of making stuff…making stuff…"

"Are you okay?"

"This weather, up and down, can't pick a fucking season. It's killing my sinuses."

"You're preaching to the snotty choir," I said. "This time of year—"

"I'm sure the pills and booze aren't helping—"

"You said you hadn't been drinking. Are you driving drunk, driving me drunk?"

"You don't wash this shit down with spring water and soda pop. But I'm wondering if I can add DayQuil on top of all of it so I can get my head clear."

"Because that's your big problem," I said under my breath.

"So I'm a little high and I've got a weird crush. I'm trying to help. You're the one who wants to kill a guy because you can't handle loose ends."

Wait. What?

"Hold up. Did I miss something?" I asked.

"You want to take care of Rickard," she said using air quotes to misrepresent what I said.

"Oh for gods sake," I said. "Your brain is compromised and you're going to—"

"Look, somebody is pulling up to our locker."

"Our locker?" I asked. "How do you know which locker—"

"Open the trunk," she said. "We need—"

"Are those men wearing wedding dresses?"

I pointed to two stocky men getting out of a plain sedan I'd seen near Posey's house. They were both wearing beaded white formal dresses and carrying shotguns.

"Aw, hell," Lindsey said. "I can't deal with this. I need to lie down."

She flopped forward and rested her head on the trunk of her cruiser. I kept an eye on the girls to see what they were going to do until Lindsey began sliding down her car and I had to catch her before she face planted into the parking lot.

"You should rest in the car," I said, trying to maneuver her back to the driver side of the cruiser. "I want to go talk to them and see — "

"Shotguns and wedding dresses," she said. "Jesus, my head is spinning."

Her body was also spinning in my grip and I was having a hard time keeping hold of her. When she started twitching I couldn't hold my grip and she fell out of my arms and onto the pavement. As I bent over to try and pick her up again, I could see the men moving around to the back of their car.

The bigger of the two, who had a bushy beard to go with his wedding dress, handed his shotgun to the other, squatter man and opened the hatchback. He pulled out a large metal box and followed the other guy to the front of the locker. Short Round looked around suspiciously while The Beard unlocked the storage locker and rolled up the door.

I wanted to know what was in that box and why the men were there and why they were wearing wedding dresses. Lindsey didn't move so I let go of her and made my way to the locker myself. It would have been easy to stay back in the safety of the car and survey the situation to see what was happening, but this way I was taking an active role. I was stirring the pot, making things happen, and I was sure I was going to be the better for it.

I was also having fun. It was a horrible thing to realize, given the violence I'd seen, and there was certain to be more violence before it was over. But as I focused on the sound of my shoes crunching on the gravel leading from the parking lot to the storage area, I felt better than I had all semester. I had a purpose, and was developing a skill set, two things that had been lacking in my life for over a year since I began final work on my thesis and began sparring regularly with Parker Farmington. I was inside the storage complex and near the locker in question when the locker exploded.

• • •

THE EXPLOSION wasn't huge, no movie-like pyrotechnics or slow motion debris flying, but it was loud. So very loud. The explosion echoed out into the parking lot and I swear it felt like the sound was knocking me to the ground and not the force of the explosion. My ears were ringing and my body was quivering and I was content right then to stay curled up in the little ball I'd curled into when I fell down.

"We need to leave," Lindsey told me.

"How did you get all the way over here so—"

"We'll take your car," she said.

"My car has a flat tire."

"Oh. Let's go get it fixed then."

"You have a person in your trunk. At least that's what I think you were about to show me before…before this."

"Jesus. So much talking. My car then. Fine. Just let's go."

I guess you could reasonably assume she was afraid to confront the eventual police presence at the crime scene with so many narcotics in her system, but the look of fear on her face was so much more intense than plain old paranoia and for the first time since I met her I was uncomfortable being with her. I stood up on my own so she would stop tugging on my shirt, but wouldn't follow her as she tried to go back to her car.

"What aren't you telling me?" I asked.

"He's the bad guy, you know that, right?"

"Who?"

"I love him anyway though. This is my situation. Him or alone for the rest of my life. I can't do that. My temper, Jesus, I'd go down for murder in a month if I didn't have someone screwing me to keep me sane."

"Is that what this is about? You want me to have sex with you?"

"I'd have more fun changing your tire myself. What is that? Is it snowing again? This weather…"

I looked into the sky and caught a thick snowflake right in the eyeball. The temperature hadn't changed much, so the snow wasn't sticking to anything, but it was still quite ridiculous how bi-polar the weather was being. If I thought about it long enough I'd find a way to link it to my current circumstances and find ways to illuminate the themes in my adventure, but the snow was wet and I wanted to get away from it so I followed Lindsey back to her car. I was still leery about throwing in with her, but the snow was falling fast in heavy, wet clumps and it was going down my back so I got into the passenger side of the cruiser.

Lindsey slammed on the gas and drove away. We were headed back the way we came going about twice as fast.

The roads were as wet as my back and the cruiser fishtailed several times without Lindsey altering her speed.

I wasn't exactly sure what time of the day it was, but I knew it wasn't late enough for it to be as dark as it was so I blamed that on the weather. That added a nice layer of low visibility over the slippery roads and it didn't take a meteorologist to figure we were in for trouble. What did surprise me was how far we made it before crashing.

We made it all the way back to the city on the expressway and were exiting at the Ambassador Bridge entrance near Mexican Town when another car flung itself in front of us from three lanes over. Lindsey's response time, dulled by drugs, booze, and I'm sure a healthy amount of shock, was fast enough to avoid hitting the car, but not without sending our car into a spin, off of the exit ramp, down into a ditch and onto its side.

"Please...my gun," she stuttered. "I can't do this anymore."

I was on the bottom with Lindsey hanging above me. My right arm was pinned underneath me but I could still feel it and took that as a triumph.

"What? No. I need you," I said. "We've got to the police."

"When they find out about..." she started. "Jesus. Please."

"Find out what?"

"Titus. What he's going to do. I can't have that on my conscious."

"Let's stop him then."

"Too late," she said. Then she vomited all over me.

CHAPTER 12

Most of Lindsey's vomit ended up on my legs; a small triumph that it wasn't all over my face, but the smell overpowered the entire car. My good hand was at a weird angle between my legs, but I was able to wiggle it to a spot where I could unhook my seat belt. When I tried to move, I was concerned less about the small triumphs I'd been cataloging because every body part I could feel hurt. A lot.

Again, the accident wasn't the sort of experience I'd been conditioned by Hollywood to expect: no explosions, no screeching metal, just the thumping of city government maintained anti-lock brakes doing their job, tires sliding across gravely snow, and the sudden dirt-muted thump of the cruiser's front end hitting the ditch and tilting the cruiser on its side like a steel omelet.

Even through pain, my brain still bubbled with useless trivia and in this instance I contemplated the rumors that drunk drivers are rarely killed when they get into accidents because the alcohol relaxes them to the point of superhuman flexibility. Whereas the people they are hitting don't see it coming so they tense up and get the ass end of gravity and perpetual motion. I certainly hadn't seen that crash coming.

I couldn't tell if the groans coming from Lindsey were of pain or more impending vomit and I really couldn't have cared less. My pain threshold had been crossed substantially more under her protection than any of the other characters I'd run into and I wanted my time with her to be done. Unfortunately, as I browsed through the rogue's gallery I'd been introduced to since I first set foot in that hardware store the night before last, I remembered the other passenger in the car.

I was able to get myself loose from my seatbelt and roll enough into the back seat to avoid the onslaught of vomit that followed. It was nothing but liquid which made me doubt her sandwich story. My only concern though was getting out of the car and away from Lindsey's mess. I'd read somewhere that the back doors of police cars can't be opened from the inside to keep prisoners from jumping out but I noticed the door was loose and figured the university had used the same penny-pinching, bottom-barrel purchasing model for their police cruisers as they did with everything else on campus. I kicked at the door with every bit of strength I could con out of my system until it popped loose.

"I'll send somebody to help," I told Lindsey, crawling

out of the car. "Keep your gun out of your mouth."

My legs were wobbly and every bit of pressure they were subjected to ached like a million leg cramps simultaneously, but I was able to hobble far enough away from the car where I didn't feel in immediate danger from Lindsey shooting at me. The temperature had dropped even more during the time I was in the car and I'd had to wiggle out of my coat to get out so I was left to the weather with only my hooded sweatshirt to keep me warm and my Converse All Stars, which were about as useful for urban hiking as they were for basketball, to get me to safety.

When I finally stopped to look around and assess my surroundings, I wondered if I might actually be closer to Canada than to where I needed to be downtown. To my left was a service drive that ran the length of the expressway for a couple of exits and would eventually wind around to the abandoned central train depot building that had been used by location scouts from every film company in Hollywood as an apocalyptic movie set, and to my right was a wide pavement field that I was pretty sure would lead to the customs area for the Ambassador Bridge crossing.

As I began walking toward where I thought the border crossing was, the snow began to clear so I could get a better view of where I was going. Just to be a bitch though, Mother Nature dropped the temperature in compensation. Every other time I'd made the trip across the bridge from this particular exit it seemed like I was at a custom's booth instantaneously after exiting the expressway.

In fact, on more than one occasion I found myself getting off at the wrong exit and not realizing it until I'd passed the point of no return and had to explain myself to un-amused booth attendants. The same trip on foot seemed to take me a frost-bitten eternity. One good thing to come of it, besides not actually succumbing to frostbite (sorry if I ruined the suspense for you), was that it helped focus my attention which was in serious need of a tune-up by that point in the day.

Each step forward was an exercise in one thousand tiny tasks that I was acutely aware of as my body screamed for mercy it would not get. My shit plans, my shit future, and all of the intervening screw-ups were pushed out of my thought path, supplanted by simple tasks like breathing and not falling down that suddenly required all of my available mental capabilities. It was this singular focus and lack of awareness of my surroundings that blindly led me nearly to the middle of a large group of people before I suddenly realized I was in the middle of a protest. I'd seen something on the news about it. A nationwide group of people with nothing better to do protesting the commercialization of Christmas and the distribution of wealth or something by blocking shipping routes. A US border seemed like a bad place for that sort of thing, what with the horror stories people tell of Homeland Security Gone Wild.

The only thing that I imagined could make the day worse

than it already was would be to be indefinitely detained without ID, which I realized was still in my coat in Lindsey's cruiser, which was sitting on its side in a ditch as the result of an accident to which I'd been a witness/participant and walked away from. That of course, led to my realization that the same car also may well have a person in the trunk and that, as the only one not there to give my side of the story, I would make a nice fall guy for whatever trouble Lindsey managed to get herself into.

These thoughts were allowed to run freely through my head because the protest crowd surrounding me was becoming progressively more agitated and aggressive in their movements and their anger warmed me. As it seemed like the group was reaching the zenith of whatever they'd been doing to get themselves all riled up, the group exploded width-wise into a human chain to block an oncoming convoy of tractor trailers.

My first thought was to throw myself in front of the lead truck and be done with this mortal world and its bullshit. This was the first time in my life I ever contemplated suicide which, considering my chosen career path, my paranoid nature, and the way my life and been circling the karmic commode lately, I found quite surprising. But in that moment I didn't see any other way out. I'd put myself into a miserable situation the first time I told my plan to Posey Wade. I had a lot of stupid ideas in the course of my day-to-day life and sometimes even made attempts to put them in motion. Telling Posey was putting it out into the world and out of my control. I can tell myself I was looking for sympathy or that I was just looking to vent, but we all know I was hoping she'd offer to help.

And she did, sort of, she gave me an out with Parker the next day that I could have used as a mulligan and been done with the whole mess. But I didn't. I let it stir and fester and let stupid fucking Parker Farmington push my buttons one more time, and now it was all out of the box. I wasn't getting it back in. Every time since then where I've tried to make it better or tried to make it go away, I only made it worse. I would go to jail. Even if I only served a few months, I'd be branded a criminal and relegated to the lowest rung of society where shit jobs and hovel apartments would be my life. But I couldn't step away from the group. I couldn't even put myself in the location to end it all. Maybe I was too optimistic to think there wasn't some way to make it all work. Or maybe suicide was just one more area that required discipline beyond what I was able to muster on any given day.

As the convoy approached, I saw a better solution flashing its lights at me. A Detroit Police Department cruiser was leading the convoy and that seemed to me a much better vehicle to throw myself in front of. I could claim to have been swept up accidentally in the protest while searching for gas or something. At worst I would be regarded as a particularly aggressive protestor and dealt with as such. I'd probably be arrested, but maybe I could get the ear of a sympathetic detective or someone with a grudge against campus cops and tell them my story. The cruiser made its way closer and the crowd began to close in on the convoy. I had no idea when the best moment would be to jump and hoped a moment of clarity would present itself.

The next few moments happened in blur of bullet points.

My hands freed from the human chain.

The blast of the cruiser's siren as it advanced on the protesters.

The cheers from behind me as I took my first steps in front of the cruiser.

Bracing for the impact.

A chorus of groans as the cruiser hit me at full speed and knocked me back to the protesters.

Then the sound of the approaching semis.

CHAPTER 13

My moment as protest hero quickly passed and the group directed their anger on my behalf by trampling over me to swarm the departing cruiser. I was able to roll around which served the dual purpose of preventing my head from getting squished by protest boots and also of assuring me I'd avoided paralysis for the second time in the last hour. A few stragglers hung back from the crowd to kick my tires and make sure I hadn't died, but nobody made any serious attempt at assistance until a commando-clad customs agent held his hand out to me.

"You can stand?"

I took his hand and pulled myself, then immediately stepped back away from him.

"The car had mostly stopped by the time it hit me," I said. "Perhaps I was a bit dramatic in my roll off."

"Come on, let's go talk."

"That's not illegal is it? I mean if anything that cop should—"

"Do you have an ID with you?"

"That seems like a dirty trick. I know technically I'm supposed to be able to show ID to any requesting law enforcement office but that's—"

"Technically," the customs commando said, "I could mace you as a threat to yourself and the public—"

"Whatever, whatever," I said. "Let's go talk. You'll like the story I have to tell."

He grunted and took a few steps before looking back to see if I was following him.

"I told you I'd go with you," I said. "I have nowhere else to go. Really."

I thought we were going to head to the concrete bunker looking building to my right, but we stopped in front of a large white pick-up truck with the US Customs logo on the side in green. The break was nice because though I had avoided a direct collision with the car, the impact had still apparently rattled my insides and I was surprised how much of my insides were necessary for standing upright.

"Up for a ride?" Commando Customs said.

I sat down on the ground next to the truck and said, "Walking hurts."

He came to my side of the truck and opened the door. I expected him to try and pick me up and lift me into the truck but he left me where I was and got into his own side of the truck. Nothing good so far had come from me getting into other people's cars, but I didn't see where I had any other choice and I imagined if this fellow had inappropriate designs on me he would have exercised them already. So I got into the truck. It took roughly as long to crawl the step and a half into the cab of the truck than it had taken me to walk from Lindsey's car to the border.

When I made it all the way into the seat I had little trouble with the seat belt and felt quite proud of myself when I clicked it in. The interior of the truck looked like a mobile version of the customs booths. The decoration theme seemed to be paperwork and coffee cups because there was a sizeable amount of both spread across both seats and the dashboard. An outdated government issue CB radio took up most of the space between the seat I was in and the driver's seat. It hummed and crackled with the comforting chatter of border activity.

My face must have hinted at the waves of nausea lapping around my brain because Custom Commando lowered my window as he pulled away. I stuck my head as far out of the window as I could and sucked in the cold air. The snow was still falling, but the flakes were smaller and more frozen as the temperature had dropped even further.

"Should I ask you for ID or something?" I asked with my head still out the window.

"You can ask. Do you want a coat or something? I've got a parka in the back?"

"Why are we heading toward the border? I don't—"

"It would really be better for both of us if you put a coat on. We should be able to get across without any trouble but—"

"We're going to Canada? I really don't have any of my ID. I left it back at…well that's part of the story I guess you're going to want to hear."

"There will be time for that later. For now, please put on the coat. You look cold."

"Fine, where is it?"

He pointed to the extended cab area that was a mess of extra clothing and tactical equipment.

"If we're going to Canada," I said, digging around looking for a coat. "I should know your name."

"Liam," he said. "But everybody calls me Buck."

I found an insulated nylon parka that seemed heavy enough to keep me warm into Canada with the window down and wriggled into it while still trying to keep my seat belt buckled.

"You don't look like a Buck," I said. "That something to do with hunting?"

He reached his arm over and tapped the embroidered name patch over the left pocket of the parka.

"Let me out please," I said when I saw the name.

"We're not close. If that's what you're worried about."

"How did you…when did…I can't even wrap my brain around—"

"She radioed from her car after the accident. She was afraid—"

"How did she know this is where I'd go?"

"We're going across now," Buck said. "Nobody should ask us anything but try to look professional."

"Like a prisoner?"

"You're not a prisoner."

"Yet," I said.

"I'm going to help you."

"That should be interesting."

"And you're going to help me."

"That should be even more interesting."

We drove across the border in silence and over the Ambassador Bridge in silence as well. I giggled a little as we passed a portable toilet off to my right about midway across the bridge. It was there every time I went over the bridge going back to my first time when I was 19. One of the first stories that really gave me trouble in my first trip through graduate school was one I tried to write about a contrarian troll who wanted to live above a bridge and set up house in the Ambassador Bridge portable toilet. But I could never get the style right and it jumped between surrealism and horror and magic realism with a healthy dose of just plain bad. Passing the toilet again made me wonder if I could dig it out again and make it work.

We made it across the Canadian side as well without trouble and pulled off to a concrete bunker that matched almost detail for detail the bunker on the US side. I waited for Buck to get out so I could follow, but he didn't move.

"There's a cab down the lot a few yards," he said. "It'll take you where you need to go."

I didn't know how to take that. I was still envisioning dark scenarios that ended with me in a secret dungeon under Windsor somewhere, but a cab was unexpected. I could see the government covering up my disappearance easily enough among their own ranks, but adding an outsider would make that harder. Buck reached into his pocket and pulled out a wad of bills and handed them over to me.

"It's not much," he said, "but it should pay for the cab and buy you a drink at the casino until you can meet with... well, I'll let that part stay a surprise for now."

"Where is she?" I asked.

"Don't worry about tipping the driver, he's a friend of mine and he'll get his later."

There was no maliciousness in Buck's tone, nothing to make me fear for my life, but I was so out of sorts by that point that I defaulted to my ongoing assumption that everyone everywhere is out to get me. But I didn't have any other choice, and I was still alive, so I got out of the truck and went down to meet the mysterious Canadian cabbie who would take me to the casino.

The cabbie was a wide blonde guy with a thin ponytail and thick body odor. He barely acknowledged me when I got in the back seat and remained silent as we took a series of back roads along the waterfront that led to the glittering Caesar's Windsor complex just across the river from Detroit. As we approached the casino I got flips of excitement in my stomach.

This would be the first clean environment I'd been in after a series of dive strip clubs, dilapidated storage facilities, and roach motel apartments. In fact, the last nice place I'd been was the Greektown casino with Posey where she conned me into getting involved with that nut job Rickard. I would know better this time. I'd be wary and cautious and on my guard. And if it all went cool, maybe I could turn all of my bad luck around with a good time at the blackjack tables.

"Hey, wasn't that the valet entrance back there?" I asked the driver when he passed by the entrance I'd used the few times I'd been to Caesar's Windsor.

"Almost."

He turned away from the main drag along the waterfront and drove toward the bar and restaurant district where 19-year-old kids came to drink legally and where women in bachelorette parties came to see full male nudity. We stopped in front of a corner establishment made up to look like an old west saloon.

"We're here," the cabbie said. "Fifteen bucks. American I guess if that's what you got."

"I don't see a casino anywhere. Is it down one of the alleys?"

"This is the place. Fifteen bucks. Tip would be nice if you

got it. Gas is a—"

"Buck said the ride was paid for," I said.

"Yeah, with the wad of cash he gave you. This ain't the first time, kid. Sometimes it's Canadian and sometimes it's American, but I always say fifteen bucks either way because I'm swell like that."

I hadn't counted the wad Buck gave me until then and I hoped there was enough to cover the ride. The bills were American and there were six of them amounting to about $100. I handed one of the twenties to the cabbie and thanked him for the ride.

I think I remember him laughing condescendingly while mentioning something about a basement. Then I remembered the rush of cold air that I initially thought was going to be the flash of energy I'd need to make it from the cab into the building but instead was the harbinger of the nauseous nail in my consciousness. I passed out in a snow bank wet and dirty from the cab's departure and wondered how it had snowed so much again without my noticing it.

Some time later I saw a large man standing over me holding a flask and a handgun.

Titus Wade said, "Dumbass" then kicked me in the groin.

CHAPTER 14

I tried to look around but my eyes were gooey with tears and blinking only seemed to make it worse. The pain was mostly gone from my gut and what little I did feel was more of the aching sort than the impending dying sort. I tried to put together a full evaluation of my surroundings and how I came to know I was talking to Titus Wade and not some random dumb thug, but man, I really didn't remember much and what I did know was cobbled together mostly through gossip and boasting from Wade himself so I wasn't even sure how much of it was true.

Early on during my initial struggles with Parker and my manuscript, I thought about writing a memoir. This was when memoirs were huge money-makers and I figured I had an interesting enough story but I could never find a way to wrap it into a narrative. All I had were random memories triggered by even more random pieces of minutiae. And those memories only served as jumping off points for more scattered memories. It was just a big jumble with no spine. But this moment with Titus and Posey stuck out to me because of its randomness.

Until that point I'd been stuck in writer mode, trying to place what was happening to me on some kind of plot chart to figure out where I was. It was like I was just watching myself as a character in a book with no control over my life and every time something happened to me I would just flip a few pages ahead to see how much longer until the end. But sitting there in the basement of a karaoke club they called The Casino, with my eyes glued shut from crying I realized there's no planning for real life.

There is no narrative spine. There are no delineated plot points to keep readers interested. There's just a random series of events triggered by even more random minutiae. I wasn't living a book. I was living a video game. Every time I looked up something was trying to shoot me or trip me or run me over. I wasn't Zelda on a quest; I was Frogger trying to get across the fucking road without getting squished. And if I survived, maybe I'd get my prize. The life I dreamed about.

And Titus Wade was the first car trying to squish me.

"How the fuck do you get in such a mess that I have to go out of the country to fix it?"

"Posey," I said.

"He's in charge," I think I heard her say.

"Shut up," Wade said. "You're kind of loopy because we needed to fix you. But clocks are ticking and we got shit to do."

"We're still in Canada?" I asked.

"Until we find him."

"Him? Who him?" I asked.

"This is bullshit," Wade said. ""You talk to him."

From the fluctuations in his voice it sounded like he was talking away from me, talking to someone else perhaps. I felt warm and cozy enough that I didn't think I was in a cell or dungeon or anything, which gave me hope that I wasn't in too deep over my head.

"Can somebody wipe my eyes?" I asked.

"I expected more vomiting," Wade said, "from what I heard about your accidents, but you cried a lot. Made me uncomfortable."

I sat up and tried to wipe my own eyes. Part of me must have expected to be restrained because I sat up with more power than I normally do and was rewarded with a trip right off of the couch and onto a battered wooden floor, hip first and then head. I don't know why I kept expecting to be in a basement office, but not only was I not in the basement of the building, I was not in an office. The couch was on a stage at the front of what looked to be a standard dive bar during the middle of the day.

"I get it," I said. "This is an elaborate performance art piece. As an artist myself I have to say—"

"Shut up Dominick," Posey said. "We all need to talk about some stuff."

"You're pretty demanding after what you did to me and who you left me with."

I tried to focus on her to my left, but I kept looking back to Titus Wade. With the goo gone from my eyes and a more focused look at him I still thought he looked strange. Granted, my only contact with him had been in the street in front of Posey's house and I'd been drunk on university-funded cocktail punch, and then one more time when he yelled at me in his office. But still, he'd seemed so much bigger. The man in front of me was certainly tall enough, but not as wide.

"He's staring at me like a queer," Wade said.

He certainly whined more than I expected Wade too.

"Who else is in this room with me?" I asked. "Is Rickard in here?"

"It's me, Dominick," Posey said, with a recognizable condescension in her voice.

"Why are you here with your brother?" I asked. "I thought you hated—"

"Jesus, Dom shut up," Posey said. "I thought we had a plan, and then you disappeared on me at the strip club."

"I met Rickard like you wanted. You left me alone. I thought it was a test."

"It wasn't a test; you should have waited for me. He listens to me." Posey said. "Now he's looking for Parker. I think he's going to kill him."

"In Canada?"

Posey shook her head.

"This is just the staging area," she said. "Big happening's going to be down in Toledo at the book festival."

"Who has a book festival in the winter?"

"The same people who have a book festival in Toledo. We can't let it get that far."

The whole thing had the potent whiff of bullshit to it, but my experiences of the previous day or so had me believing anything was possible. I could be convinced that Posey was genuinely interested enough in Parker's well-being to go after Rickard but I didn't have the same faith in her brother

"What's he have planned for Parker?" I asked, pointing to Titus.

"Titus is going to help us. We don't have much time."

She continued explaining to me what an asset he was going to be but I lost focus as the cumulative effects of my ordeal caught up with me.

"Is it getting really hot in here?" I asked.

"Dominick, are you okay? You don't look very well."

"Titus was a paramedic for a while," Posey said. "He looked you over after you collapsed outside and didn't see anything traumatic."

"I think it's more shock than anything else," I said as Titus put his hands on me and moved them around in a surprisingly competent way.

I thought I might need x-rays or surgery or something for

internal injuries, but if this was as close to a doctor as I was going to get for the time being then I was going to let him do it unhindered.

"You mumbled something about a car accident," Posey said.

"Two. I flipped in Lindsey's car, and then I was hit by a cop car at the border."

"Lindsey," Posey said. "Hmmph."

"So what now?" I asked.

"We wait for Parker."

"Here?"

"There's a couple of single occupancy rooms upstairs, and we think he might be staying in one of them but we can't get anyone to confirm it."

"Where do we hide?"

"Us: upstairs in the other room," she said. "You: down here in plain sight. Do you want to be a bartender or do you want to DJ the karaoke?"

"Won't he recognize me?"

"Maybe, maybe not. I don't think he'll take you seriously either way. But you can signal us when he's here. Now drink or sing?"

"Sing. I guess."

I tried to say it with as much false modesty as I could muster, but while I enjoyed drinking, I was awful at mixing drinks. Singing though, that's my thing. Especially on a stage. Especially undercover. I didn't even mind when the first singer to volunteer was a drunken frat boy who wanted to duet Elton John with me.

"You be George Michael," he said.

CHAPTER 15

I'd been a DJ all of ten minutes before someone threw liquor at me. Posey and Titus were upstairs preparing some sort of trap while I, the dangling worm, was paying too much attention to scanning the door and the window looking outside to the street corner to concentrate on my performance. My preferred voice range runs toward country music or similar crooners like Elvis or Roy Orbison, which normally goes over well at the blue collar bars I'd sang at before. But the piece-meal audience of late-lunchers and middle shift folks drinking before work were having none of it and one of them took his protest to the air.

What I didn't know was that the shot glass whizzing a breathe away from my left ear would set in motion a series of decisions in the part of my brain that hadn't been scrambled by my recent stunt work with cars. I was mildly aware of the decisions as I had told my own self that the guy who threw the shot glass didn't look like the miniature glassware wielding sort and that if I really thought about it what he looked like to me was a cop and of the random people collected in that bar, a cop still stuck out and made me wonder why he was there.

While I was wondering, and also trying not to butcher a too-high rendition of Neil Diamond's "Brother Love's Traveling Salvation Show", my brain was doing its own scheming. So when I saw Parker Farmington through the window to the street, instead of announcing a free round of drinks on the house—the code I'd been instructed to give by Titus and Posey in the hopes of causing a distraction—I dropped the mike on the stage like a pissed off rock star and ran out to meet Parker before he entered the bar.

"It's a trap," I said, plowing into Parker to get him out of the bar's doorway and back into the thick of street traffic on the sidewalk. None of the businesses in the city must have allowed smoking because every building had a little thicket of bundled up smokers in front. Parker stumbled back into one of these thickets and went down with a thud.

"Dammit," he said.

He stared at me without saying anything else and I looked around for a cab to grab. Instead, I heard a horn honk behind me and saw a battered sedan that I assumed had been waiting as part of the trap. I jumped in the backseat dragging Parker with me and didn't get as much of a look from the driver as I expected.

"I'm a friend of Titus and Posey," I said. "There's been a change in plans."

Parker still had his legs hanging out of the car and I couldn't close the door. I briefly wondered if I had injured him when I knocked him to the ground. In the second or two it took me to finally get Parker fully into the car, Titus appeared and jumped into the front seat. We drove away without anyone giving chase but that didn't stop the driver from weaving down alleys and one way streets like he was auditioning as a stunt man. We finally stopped ten blocks away, on the edge of the main downtown district that would loop back around to the Canadian side of the bridge if you followed the signs. We were in the parking lot of a strip mall that was vacant except for a small pawn shop and a Canadian franchise of Little Caesar's pizza that looked stuck in the 1980s.

"Get out," Wade said.

"Parker and I have some business first."

I reached into my pocket and pulled out what was left of the wad of cash Buck had given me and pushed it over the back of the seat toward Titus then turned back to Parker.

"I didn't know what I really wanted the last time we talked," I said. "I was in a rough place with some crazy ideas but now I know what I want. What I need you to help me with. If you'll just sign my form."

Parker continued staring at me without saying anything.

Titus flipped through the wad of bills but was apparently

still paying attention to my conversation.

"What kind of form?" He asked.

"For school. For a novel I wrote. I want to go to New York City and write."

Titus stopped counting and looked back at me.

"Novel, huh? Is it any good?"

"It's finished. That's all it needs to be," I said. "And Parker here needs to sign the goddam form that says it meets the qualifications of graduation, which are only that it's finished."

Titus put his arm on the back of the seat and rested his head on it.

"I wrote a book too," he said. "Not a novel though. I like poetry. Drawn from the streets. That's my stuff. Like a letter to my job saying *fuck you* only in better language, you know?"

"Does he look alright to you? I think I might have hurt him."

Titus held up the wad of bills.

"This isn't enough."

"It's all I've got."

He looked back and the money and squeezed it into a ball then rustled it around in his hand before looking back to me.

"Tell you what," he said.

Then he looked at the driver and then back to me.

"I'll stay here and get a cab. Dave here will take you back to the hotel so you two can do what you need to do."

"Does Dave have a gun?"

"Dave is from New Jersey, he doesn't need a fucking gun."

I pointed my finger at Parker who rolled his eyes.

"Who's going to point a gun at his head then and make him sign my form?"

Wade got out of the car and waved for me to follow him. "Come around back here, let me show you something."

He went to the back of the car and opened the trunk.

"You're not going to put me in there," I said.

"Why would I do that? I got other shit in here more important than you."

The trunk really was full. Of books. Boxes of books. It reminded me of what Posey had said about him planning something for the book festival in Toledo. That put what he had just told me about his poetry writing in a new context. While I was contemplating the books, Titus pulled a shotgun out of a duffel bag that was shoved between two of the boxes and held it out for me.

"Are those your poetry books?" I asked.

Titus snapped open the gun and shook out one of the shells and put it in my hand.

"Rubber," he said.

"Is this some kind of sex thing?"

"You seem twitchy. With these loaded in the gun you could shoot him in the head and not kill him."

I rolled the shell around on my fingers and shook it a little.

"Really? In the head?"

Titus took the shell back from me and reloaded it into the gun then handed it back to me. I held it like a toddler holding a wriggling puppy and he moved my hands into a less offensive positioning.

"Maybe some bruising or contusions," he said. "But nobody should die. So let's go. Now."

I swung the gun up into firing position.

"Just me," I said, and fired.

I aimed for his chest but hit him in his gut. The recoil of the weapon snapped my shoulder back and sent a wad of pain through the left side of my body. But I kept my composure as best as I could and was able to get back into the car and crawl over the driver's side when Dave the Driver got out to check on Titus. I peeled away and didn't stop driving for another hour when I got off of the 401 at a rest area and freaked out. I cried and giggled and covered almost every other emotion, though surprisingly, did not vomit. Parker was still out of it and sprawled in the backseat and I was at a loss for what to do next. I had what I wanted. I had the man who needed to sign my form, a gun with which to persuade him to sign the form, and an empty area in a foreign country where I could dump him after he signed it. I had everything I needed.

Except the form.

At some point I had left my backpack with the form tucked into my black leather X-Men folio behind and hadn't remembered to take the form with me. That revelation still didn't make me vomit, but I did cry a lot more. Especially when I remembered where I probably left the backpack. In the crazy woman's van I'd ridden in with Rickard. If I could find her though, she also had that big bag of money with her.

CHAPTER
16

had to smack Parker to finally wake him up. He sat up and rubbed his head and then his groin.

"Did you rape me?"

"I poked you with a shotgun to make sure you weren't dead."

"So you could bring me out here and kill me?"

"Do you even know where we are?"

"You don't seem smart enough to get across the border with an unconscious person in your backseat so I'd guess we're still in Canada."

"A rest stop in Canada to be specific."

"I'm hungry. Do I get a last meal?"

"I'm not going to kill you," I said. "I am hungry though. Do you have any money? I spent all mine on the shotgun."

"That's not much of a plan."

"I've had to improvise. How much money do you have?

I can pay you back when we get back in the US."

I looked at him in my rear view mirror and watched him reach for his wallet. He stared at it for a long time without opening it. This was the first time I'd seen him freaked out and I suspected it had something to do with the time he spent in Titus Wade's care.

"What did he do to you?" I asked.

"You want tips?"

"We're in this together whether you believe it or not. They're going to be coming for both of us and it would help—"

"You didn't save me. I can see where you're going, but don't think you saved me."

It sounded like empty bravado, and just the fact he thought he needed to point out that there was even the possibility I might have saved him from Titus Wade gave me enough of a happy buzz that I didn't push the issue. I also was really hungry and he was my own source of cash at that time and I didn't want to jeopardize that.

"How much do you have in your wallet?"

"I don't know, a couple hundred dollars," he said, then paused for a long breath before continuing. "Where is he anyway?"

"We're not saved from anything," I said. "We're screwed, down the road. Both of us. They'll come for us and we'll see what happens, but for now let's look for some food. Really, $200 dollars is what you have on you?"

He shrugged his shoulders and laid his head against the window of his door.

"I don't like credit cards and I don't ever want to not be able to buy something small I want because I don't have money on me."

"I think up the road is a Tim Horton's," I said. "Drive-thru is probably our best bet to go undetected."

"How long has it been?"

"I had it just the other day. Well, maybe about a week ago. They have one over by—"

"How long has it been since you kidnapped me?"

"We left Windsor about an hour ago," I said, trying very hard not to argue his use of the word kidnapping.

True as it might be.

"Where are we headed?"

It was my turn to shrug.

"Away from Windsor I guess. That's where the trouble was and I knew I couldn't get back over the border so I drove the other way as far as could before I started thinking about what else needed to happen."

"Which is?"

Another shrug while I explained everything that had happened so far as it related to him and me. The key points were that I was stuck in the country without ID, possibly facing murder charges for Rickard or at least facing questions about his death, and also facing the retribution of Titus and Posey Wade who were already in the country, and Lindsey

Buckingham and Morton Taylor, Jr. who would probably be in the country soon.

"Niagara Falls," he said. "Maybe three hours along this highway. It's the perfect story for getting back in."

"We're on our honeymoon?"

"Casinos. Two of them now. We say we had some bad luck in Windsor and decided to try our luck at the new Niagara Falls casino."

"I don't have ID. Even the most lax border guard needs to look at something."

"You'll ride in the trunk then. I have a fast pass for easy border crossing and I've never had them stop me, let alone look in the trunk."

"Why do you spend so much time in Canada?'

"I still don't like you and I still think you're an idiot and I don't want to talk to you. Yes, we're stuck together, you're right about that but this isn't a buddy picture okay?"

"What if they've put a block on your fast pass? They had the connections to get me into the country, why would they be able to use those connections to block us from getting out?"

"They have a very good Dijon mustard for the sandwiches at Tim Horton's in the US and it's nicely complimented by their coffee and the chocolate glazed donuts that come with the combo meal. I would very much like some of that right now."

"Food then, fine. We can talk while we eat."

"Not with our mouths full."

I turned around in my seat and looked directly into Parker Farmington's eyes.

"I have a shotgun you foul, puny little man. You'll answer whatever goddam questions I ask and you'll keep your mouth shut when I'm not talking to you. Otherwise I'll tie you to one of these kilometer markers and call Titus Wade and tell him where to find you. I know you're terrified of him. I am too, but I'm too hopped up on my own stupidity and so far successful incompetence that it doesn't matter."

"Regular coffee then," he said. "Decaf doesn't seem like it will cut it today."

We drove another fifteen minutes in complete silence before I saw the next sign for a Tim Horton's. I ordered for both of us and paid with money Parker gave me. He asked for extra packets of the Dijon mustard and I ordered three donuts. At the next rest stop we pulled off the highway again to eat.

When his sandwich was gone, Parker said, "Our biggest enemy is going to be this ridiculous speed limit."

"The last time I drove this way was on the way to Toronto with a friend of mine after he had just graduated college. He wanted to circle the whole—"

"They may have friends at the Windsor border, but they can't risk putting it out wide because they'd have to explain to a lot of people why they want us and that doesn't look good for them."

"Eventually it will all catch up with us."

"Eventually, yes," Parker said. "By which time we'll be back in the US, probably in Buffalo or Cleveland where we can hide and regroup without threat of international incident."

"I've never been to Buffalo," I said.

I finished the last bits of my sandwich and my last donut, thinking about Buffalo. The truth was I hadn't been very many places at all and Buffalo seemed as exotic to me as Paris. When we were back on the road, it was a delicate balance to keep the car topped out at the maximum speed limit without going over. We couldn't risk even a modest investigation by an officer if we were pulled over.

"This car," I said. "We're going to need to get rid of it."

"I don't know how to steal a car."

"You're legitimate, maybe you can rent one."

"True, true. Why draw attention to ourselves needlessly. I guess it will be a good way to test ourselves too. If we can't rent a car, we'll never be able to cross the border. And if we do get into trouble, we'll only need to deal with small time police around here, not Homeland Security. Brilliant Dominick."

And there it was. It only took an illegal border crossing, threats of violence, and drive thru meals on the run to finally get the validation I'd been craving from Parker Farmington. It wasn't related to my novel, but that would come in time. I had to believe that Parker's problems with my novel had more to do with him not liking me as a person. Because if he had no problems with me personally that only left the novel at fault and I wasn't ready to deal with that just then.

"Thanks," I said, trying not to let the giggle through in my voice.

"So how about you put that shotgun in the trunk and take a rest while I drive?"

I was in no shape to be driving and welcomed the idea of a break. Had my insides not been beaten like a dive gym speed bag and my legs not taken a whack from the hood of a police cruiser, I may have declined the offer for fear of giving control to the man I was still technically holding as my prisoner. But full-blown paranoia took energy and passion I wasn't able to muster. So I pulled off to the side of the road and put the shotgun in the trunk and was about to get back in the car when I thought again about the boxes of books in the trunk. I had just stowed the shotgun back in the duffel bag and was pulling a book out of the box closest to me when a police cruiser pulled off the side of the road behind us and flashed its lights.

CHAPTER

17

I dropped the book back into the box, but didn't move much else of my body. The police officer was still in his cruiser and hadn't made contact with us yet. He or she was most likely running the sedan's plates through their system to see if any flags popped up. I knew police officers did that all the time, even on routine stops with no reason to expect trouble. It's how most criminals were caught. So just because a cop stopped didn't mean trouble yet.

It was such a strange day running into situations I never would have expected to be in and running into them more than once. That was the second time I found myself waiting for a police officer to approach me while I was in a compromising possibly criminal position. I was more comfortable, relatively speaking, riding shotgun with Parker than I had being with Morton Taylor Jr. who would have most likely murdered the cop if it had been anyone other than Lindsey.

This time I was quite confident that the cop was not going to be Lindsey and that no one was going to be murdered. The worst case scenario, and it certainly was an awful scenario, was that the car would be flagged stolen and we'd be arrested by provincial troopers and taken to a Canadian jail where our options would be minimal, but workable. I couldn't come up with a good scenario.

"Good afternoon officer," I said when I saw him get out of his car.

He was still putting his hat on as he walked slowly toward us.

"Is everything all right here, sir?"

"Fine, just looking for something in the trunk. Are we... is there something you need from us?"

He was still near his car and stayed where he was while we chatted. His hands weren't near his gun and I took that as a sign that he didn't view me as a danger yet.

"Anyone else in the car?"

"My friend Parker is in the driver's seat. Did we do something wrong?"

"We got a call about some car trouble along this road," he said.

"I don't think that was us. We just pulled off a minute or two ago."

"Why was that?"

"I needed to look for something in the trunk. When I start

obsessing about something I can't let it go until I take care of it. Was kind of making my friend nervous."

The officer still didn't move from his spot and gave me a full look over. I've never been one to look natural at any given time, especially not when I need to the most, but I must not have done anything to register as an immediate threat to the officer, myself or the public good, because he eventually relaxed his stance and began backing toward his car.

"Just be careful on these shoulders here," he said. "Couple days in a row people have been killed while changing tires around this area."

"Thanks. I think we're all set here so we're just going to get back on the road."

"Aren't you going to get what you were looking for?"

Crap. That's what always happens. I've seen enough episodes of reality cop shows to know it's always the small detail that screws everything up. But wait. An idea.

"Wasn't in there," I said. "He was right. It's going to make him impossible to ride with now."

"Have a good day. Drive safe."

I didn't let out my breath until the cop was in his car and had pulled completely away from us. When I finally exhaled, I found out I'd been holding more than my breath because I peed myself as well.

"You smell like my mother's house," Parker said when I got into the car.

"Apparently I urinate on myself when I get nervous. Do

you still want to drive?"

He nodded and got out of the car and came around to my side of the car.

"I heard you tell the police officer I was the one driving."

"In case he asked for my ID."

"We're in enough trouble we've created for ourselves," Parker said. "We don't need any additional trouble from lying."

I nodded my understanding and set my head back against the seat and closed my eyes to think about our next move. When I woke up we were in the parking lot of a motel looking over an empty concrete swimming pool. It was dark outside, but the parking lot was well lit. The whole area I could see around us, in fact, was very brightly lit in the way only a garish tourist trap city can be lit. I'd never been to Niagara Falls, but I'd been to enough little cities like it to recognize the glow.

"We're here already?"

"You slept a lot," Parker said, "which you seemed to need."

I nodded again. My neck was stiff as was the rest of my body. But my head felt okay in general and my focus seemed to be clearer than it had been the rest of the day.

"How long has it been?" I asked.

"Since I started? Almost five hours. There was traffic nearly right away. Possibly related to the other car on the side of the road our police friend mentioned."

"We're staying here then?"

"Not overnight. But that police stop was interesting for us, and I think it means good things."

"Because the car wasn't reported stolen?"

He nodded again. I think both of us had been through enough that left us incapable of complex verbal exchanges. Maybe that would be good for me because I would say less that I would regret. I very rarely regret nods.

"I wouldn't be surprised," he continued slowly, "if they came after us here."

"Why are we waiting to cross then? We can be across within the—"

"We can't keep running from them. We've got a start, some space for thinking, that's why we're here. I don't want to run from them."

"You want to fight them?"

"There's something about those books you might not know. I heard Titus talking about it with his driver."

"They contain hidden code for a treasure map?"

Parker sighed and clenched his hands on the steering wheel.

"This," he said, drawing the word out until he came comically close to sounding like the snake from the Jungle Book. "This is why your plotting has problems. You're lazy. You go for the easy joke, the easy solution."

"I can't believe you're using this situation to rip on my writing. We have bigger things to worry about than my preference for—"

"This is all about your writing."

"Whatever," I said, choking back my own similar feelings that I refused to acknowledge in his judgmental presence.

"You've mortgaged your entire identity on being a writer and when that investment didn't look to be paying off you took the easy way out. Instead of examining the foundation of your investment to figure out why it wasn't paying off, you looked to blame someone else."

"That's not fair."

"I agree. I'm in a foreign motel parking lot on the run from a thug bounty hunter you set on me because I had the audacity to push you to be a better writer. That's not fair."

"Titus didn't come after you because of me."

"Not this time, I know. But you wanted to. And you made your stupid move back at the bar because you felt bad about it and thought you got me into trouble. But again, you were only looking at it from your point of view."

I got out of the car because I didn't feel like hearing my own insecurities about my career spit back in my face by my mortal enemy. My first foot gripped the concrete of the parking lot nicely but my second foot found a patch of ice and took all of me for a ride to the ground. When my head stopped ringing and I looked up, I saw Parker standing over me. I was almost relieved to see him finally making his escape. He'd leave me here to be picked up by the police and I could finally end my charade and see what life had left for me. He put his foot on my chest and I waited for him to pull the shotgun on me.

Instead he said: "You didn't save me. You fucked up my plan. I was going to take Titus Wade for a lot of money and you fucked it all up."

He punctuated each of the last four words with a stomp on my chest.

"He was setting you up," I said.

"I was keeping him close," Parker said with another stomp to my chest. "And having sex with Posey. She told me about the hot tub. The naked hot tub."

"Fuck."

"But you can still help me. We're going to let them come here to us, because we have his books and he really needs those books, and you're going to help me."

"Help you attack and blackmail Titus Wade?

"Yes."

CHAPTER 18

Parker Farmington laid his plan out for me and it was surprising in its simplicity and workability. We were sitting at a back corner booth in the diner attached to the Barrel Roll Inn and he was about to tell me why the books in the trunk of our stolen car were so goddam important.

"It's poetry, yes, but it's based on reality," he said.

"How based?"

Parker pushed a copy of the book over to me and held it open to a page in the middle. It was a haiku about a drug dealing biker snitch.

"No," I said.

"Posey and I figured it out together after the last time he caught us together."

"The language is really quite beautiful. I'm a little jealous."

"And the subject is very much real. Well, was real until

somebody found out what he was doing and set him on fire."

I flipped through the rest of book and scanned the poems. The styles varied across the full spectrum from sonnets to the last section, which was an epic poem about a crooked border guard, his sister, and a destitute bounty hunter.

"These are true?"

"Who would think that thugs and lowlifes would read poetry and understand it, let alone recognize each other?"

A waitress interrupted our conversation with a soft grunt and a snap of gum. She looked like a reject from a John Waters flick and smelled like the grease trap of a deep fryer. She stared at me, waiting for me to answer a question she hadn't bothered to ask.

"Coffee," Parker said. "For both of us. Black."

He turned to me.

"Black right?" he asked.

I nodded.

"Whiskey keeps it black, eh?" I said.

"And a platter of the regular stuff for both of us to pick at."

"Tell me about the storage locker," I said when the waitress left. "Tell me everything. Did you know two guys in wedding dresses went to that same locker today and blew it up? One of them was killed."

Parker's face went loose as if he was dropping his jaw, but not letting his mouth open to reveal it. His eyes were the only thing expanding and his brows arched upward as his facial muscles dropped.

"Your money wasn't in the locker either," I continued. "Did you know that?"

"What money?"

"I know about your book deal with the publisher who wants to mix the blood of your subject with the—"

"He's not my subject. And the blood thing was just a…it wasn't really going to happen."

"And the money?"

"You don't have it," he said. "Or you'd be gone from here."

"I know who has it. The same person has my backpack with my thesis form in it. The thesis form you're going to sign."

"We'll see about that," he said. "First we need to get on the phone to Titus and find out what he's got in his head about me and where I am."

"You think they still have pay phones in Niagara Falls? It seems kind of stuck in time here."

"We'll use your cell phone. It doesn't matter if they recognize the number because—"

"I don't have a cell phone."

"You don't have it with you?"

"I don't have one at all," I said. "I can't qualify credit-wise and I'm not really fond of them to begin with. I'd still be using a typewriter if I could take it into coffee shops with me. We'll have to use yours."

He didn't answer me right away. I suspected it was because he didn't have one for the same reasons I didn't have one and he was about as comfortable acknowledging our similarities as I was.

"I don't have one either," he said. "We'll call from the desk at the hotel. I know the desk clerk and—"

"You what?"

"I've been here before. I've been here often and I like to—"

"Are you a Canadian gambling addict?"

"Why doesn't matter. I come here enough to know people that can help us."

"This could have all happened much sooner and we could be in one of these rooms now, taking hot showers or drinking cheap liquor from the pink brick store over there or we could just be lying down. I've been banged around a lot today and I took an uncomfortable nap in an uncomfortable car…"

I said more stuff after that, but stopped listening to myself when Parker got up from his side of the table and came over to me. He grabbed me by the back of the collar and snapped my torso backward and then to the side, smack into the paneled wall. A neon clock advertising Canadian whiskey that the diner didn't sell fell on my head and I started to laugh.

"I come here because of cancer you miserable little puke. Cancer treatment and cancer drugs, cheap cancer treatment and cheap cancer drugs."

I picked the clock up off of the seat next to me and tossed it over to where Parker had been sitting. It took powers of restraint I didn't know I was capable of to keep from smacking him back with it.

"Were you an asshole before the cancer or did it make you that way?"

Parker went back to his seat and threw the clock one more booth over and folded his hands on the table between us.

"It's not exactly new for me, but it's more...acute...lately."

"Are you dying?"

"Probably."

"Family?"

"Dead, mostly. Some of them are out west. They don't care for me."

"Because you're an asshole?"

"We can get a room," Parker said. "You can rest while I make the call and get some drinks."

"Why are you being so nice?"

"Because I'm exhausted and this is easier."

I wanted more rest too so I went with it. The motel gave us an actual physical key to the room, but to protect our security the key didn't have our room number on it. The desk clerk, an enormous Arab man with effeminate features and a bald head, scribbled our room number on the back of a business card for a local freak museum and sent us on our way.

The motel was a U-shaped building with two floors and

the empty pool and parking lot as the center of it all. Our room had a giant picture window right next to the door that looked out on the pool in all its glory.

"You'd think they thought this view was on par with the falls," I said.

"Watch TV or whatever, I'm going to go get some wine. Is that acceptable to you, do you know how to drink wine?"

"I can fake it. I'll probably be asleep anyway."

After Parker left I craved a long hot shower but I couldn't keep myself upright long enough and settled at the back of the tub while the hot water pulverized my skin. I'm not sure about the exact timeline of the events that followed, but sometime after I fell asleep under the water, the hotel desk clerk and the waitress from the diner broke into the hotel room wearing wedding dresses and started shooting.

CHAPTER 19

The desk clerk fired five times at me and hit the sink, the floor in front of him, the wall behind me, and the wall to my left. I was no ballistics expert, but from the look of the small gun in his giant hand and the minimal damage the hits were inflicting, I guessed he was using a small caliber pistol like the ones my cousins up north used to shoot moles, squirrels, rats, and each other. The waitress, in a wedding dress disturbingly similar to the desk clerk's, had a small gun in her hand as well, but wasn't using it.

I was too tired and sore and disoriented to do much in the way of dodging the shots, but the desk clerk's aim seemed to do most of the work for me. When his gun finally ran out of bullets, the waitress raised hers. Before she could fire, I flopped out of the bathtub and ran as fast as I could in a squat out of the bathroom and out of the room. They'd been kind enough to leave the door hanging open when they came in so I was able to get out in a hurry. I almost ran into Parker who was coming toward me along the narrow breezeway.

He was able to dance out of our collision which put him square in a tangle with the desk clerk and the waitress on their way out of the room in pursuit. All three of them went down in an ugly, ill-fashioned scrum and I spun back around and used the opportunity to dive on top of them all and go for the guns. I threw the clerk's gun over the railing into the parking lot while Parker struggled to get a bottle of wine out of the plastic grocery bag he was carrying.

I got the waitress's gun at roughly the same time Parker got his bottle free. He cracked the desk clerk across the head with his bottle and I put my knee in the waitress's chest and the gun to her head.

"Who sent you?" I asked.

She must have sensed my awkwardness with the gun and wasn't threatened because instead of answering me she lunged at me. I tried to kick her but twisted my ankle and flopped to the ground. The waitress kept flying forward over me and over the railing landing on the concrete below next to the empty swimming pool.

"For a cancer patient," I said, "you're freakishly strong."

"Adrenaline," he wheezed. "It's wearing off though. We should leave."

"I need to hit the can first."

I've always had a small bladder and, like my need for sleep, it tended to affect me at the most inopportune times.

"Wonderful language," Parker said. "I'll get the car. Don't dawdle."

I knew I shouldn't have let him out of my sight, but this was my first successful kidnapping in only two attempts and I was focused entirely on the feeling of relief as every bit of food and drink I'd consumed since my last trip to the bathroom exited my body like a gulf coast city fleeing a hurricane. When I went back to where the car should have been I realized that it didn't matter how many times my bladder did me right, all it took was one time to screw me over. Without Parker and his fast pass I had no transportation, no ID, and no allies, such as they were. I also lost Parker again and along with that, lost my chance to keep him close until I could get the form back for him to sign.

I could have tried to get across the border on my own, and when they arrested me try to get them to contact Buck, or just give myself up and let the chips fall where they may. But I'm an optimistic person and won't count myself out until all of the options are off the table and the game is called. So I went back to the hotel room and continued with the plan Parker had put in motion and waited for Titus or Posey to call the room. It could have been a fool's errand and Parker may not have even made any calls, but I figured Parker's call was what had triggered the attack. So I waited.

Three hours later I was watching a horror movie on cable about a haunted hunting lodge that ate people with a lake or something when Titus and Posey Wade showed up. Posey made a run and flopped on top of me. It felt nice until she started punching me. Titus let her wail on me for a bit before he pulled her off of me and held her at bay with one meaty arm.

"Parker left a while ago," I told him.

"Where's my car?" Titus asked.

"Did you send two people in wedding dresses to kill us?"

Posey popped up from the floor and hung on my words. I couldn't figure out what her deal was. She wasn't the Posey I knew from class, and she wasn't even the slightly more manipulative Posey from the hot tub. She had the blank look and poor motor skills of a drunk, but there was no slurring in her words and I didn't smell any alcohol on her.

"New wedding dresses or more vintage styles?" she asked.

"I was in the bathtub," I said, pointing to the bathroom. "Letting the hot water burn away my aches and pains. And I fell asleep. One of them was a man in a wedding dress and he shot at me."

"But did you see—"

"You want to see the dress? Fine. Come here."

I rolled off of the bed away from Posey and went to the bathroom and tried to open the door. The door opened a crack but I couldn't get it open so I glanced back at Titus and waved him over.

"A little help?" I said.

"I want my shotgun back too," he said, pushing and

shoving the door open.

"It's in the trunk of your car," I said, "with your books."

Titus shoved me away from the bathroom hard enough to make me stumble and fall. From my position I could see Posey lying on the floor as well.

"Why are you helping him?" I asked Posey, rolling onto my side. "I thought you loved Parker because he's such a beautiful fucking writer about baseball and architecture and—"

"The dresses are important," she said. "You'll be lucky to have Titus with you."

"What's his deal with Canada? He mentioned something about cancer and coming here for cheap drugs but it all seems so much more sinister than that."

The bathroom door opened before Posey could answer me and Titus stepped out over the body of the desk clerk. Titus was still in the process of zipping up his pants as he came toward us. Posey was on her feet, smoothing out the messed up bedding where I'd been watching television earlier. I was still on the floor and uninspired to change my position.

"I stole your car and stole your prisoner," I said. "Whatever you're going to do to me, don't make me wait for it."

Wade was looking through the closet and then the pressboard dresser drawers. He didn't face me at all when he spoke.

"Maybe a smack or two would be nice, but my sister speaks highly of you. Mostly."

"You could have gone after Parker yourself," I said. "You don't need me."

"It's not about you and my brother or my brother and Parker," Posey said. "This is my brother and Rickard."

Titus came up empty in the closet and the drawers as well as under the bed and one more time in the bathroom when he finally dragged the desk clerk's body into the main room.

"In survival scenarios you don't always know what you'll need or when you'll need it," Titus said. "So you learn to recognize what might be helpful in the future and hold onto it and keep an eye out for a good use."

"So I'm like a potion or a key in a role playing game?"

"Unless you want me to store you in the bed of my truck, don't ever talk like that again around me."

CHAPTER 20

"You're not going to like this," Titus said. "We've got to go back down through Detroit."

"I thought we might."

Posey was asleep in the slim back seat of Titus's truck and I was riding shotgun. I kept trying to get a good look at Titus as he drove without being too creepy. I wasn't having much of a problem, because his thoughts were clearly somewhere other than where I was. He didn't have the squinty, furrowed look of someone with trouble on his mind; he looked more like people have told me I look when I'm daydreaming about a story idea. I had a lot of questions for Titus, but as a fellow writer I wanted to respect his creative space. So I looked out my own window and thought about my own story.

My current adventure had crossed into territory I could no longer wrap any kind of believable narrative structure around, which was freeing in a sense. Other than bad dialogue and clichéd characters, one of the biggest problems with stories I'd heard in writing workshops was the writer adhering too close to real life events. Real life has a crappy narrative style with a sense of irony that would be intolerable to the general reader. Characters in real life have random motives and few, if any, underlying themes in their lives.

So, freed from trying to put the last two days in context, I dreamed of a new story completely. Being around Titus Wade and Morton Taylor and Posey was enough to dislodge the criminals and bounty hunters and strippers and degenerates from my imagination. Instead I mulled an inspirational love story about a pair of wild child country singers who move back to the small town where they grew up to reconnect after they have a baby.

It was the kind of sappy stuff I liked to read and watch as a teenager and into my early college years but had no interest in after Melissa lost our baby and then I lost Melissa. My thoughts then bailed on fiction entirely and I pondered what I'd had with Melissa and what could have been. It was the first time in a long time I could remember thinking about my life in a positive context without it being anchored to writing. Maybe I was growing up for real.

"I read your poetry," I said, "The books that were in the trunk. Is that really your stuff?"

"I've spent a decade of my life trying to sort shit out because I can't journal normally like my therapist wanted me to."

"Parker was telling me—"

"Parker Farmington has an asshole for a mouth and should keep it shut."

"There's something, I don't know—kindred—in your style."

"That's bullshit."

I rubbed my hands on my knees to get my circulation flowing.

"Does it have to be so cold in here?"

"You're not the only tired who's tired."

I hoped I would pass out and sleep through the rest of the trip, but I was awake for every slow-moving, dark, boring kilometer. My mind and body perked up when we cruised back into Windsor's downtown area because I knew I was going to have to be on my game for the border crossing. I watched the buildings as we went by the casino and along the grimy pathways along the bridge footings, and when we came to the plaza for Customs I looked at Titus again.

"Do I get to know what the plan is or are we improvising?"

"You don't improvise with border patrol. You keep your mouth shut, you look everyone in the eye and act like everything is a-okay."

"Because it is, right? You've done what you need to do, paid who you need to pay. Right? This is why we—"

"That's not acting like everything is cool. That's acting like a fool."

He leaned across my body and opened the glove box.

There were five or six prepaid cell phones sealed in plastic and he pulled one of them out and tossed it on my lap then slammed the glove box shut.

"Open that, would ya?"

I didn't have a knife or scissors or any sharp object except my keys. My parents' house was the longest and sharpest of the few keys on my ring so that's the one I used. As I was hacking at the plastic, I thought about what it represented that I still had a key to my parents' house. By itself the fact that I had a key wasn't strange. A number of my friends who lived on their own had keys to their parents' houses for emergency purposes. But mine represented a security chain that was always going to hold me back from taking the big risks needed for the big life I wanted to lead.

I used to tell myself I would be able to take the big risks because if I failed, I would always have a place to go and recover. What it really did was hold me back, because when faced with a choice between a single room hovel and ketchup diet in New York City or my comfy room at home with free meals, I always chose the comfy room. One of the big reasons I'd never pursued a screenwriting career was because I was terrified of moving across the country without my safety net if I failed.

There's also the self-esteem component. I didn't trust my skill enough to keep me employed in a lifestyle that would match what I had at my parents' house, and I wasn't willing to sacrifice my standard of living to subsist on the lowly income level my writing would provide. This could have been a great moment to break free of that chain and pull the key off and throw it out the window, because I knew if I was caught illegally crossing the border or confronted with any of the other numerous misguided deeds from the last 48 hours, that life and that safety net would be gone anyway.

But I didn't. I kept cutting at the plastic until it opened and I handed the phone over to Titus. He made a broad motion of putting his arms in the air so he didn't touch the phone. It bounced off his thigh and onto the floor between his legs. I leaned over and searched with my right hand until I felt the phone and grabbed it. Back upright I turned the phone on and waited for further instructions. Titus didn't say anything. I looked back at Posey but she was still sleeping.

"Who do I call?" I asked.

"Text," he said, and then read me off a series of numbers.

I tried to type in the numbers but was having trouble. Titus pulled off to the side of the street and slammed on the brakes. He grabbed the phone from me and typed out a message like a pro then dumped the phone in the cup holder between us when he was done. We made a U-turn and left the auto plaza and pulled into the parking lot of yet another Tim Horton's.

The phone beeped and vibrated in the cup holder. Titus picked it up, looked at it, then put it back in the glove box and smacked me on the leg, and then he nodded at Posey who was still sleeping.

"Wake her up. It's time to cross."

CHAPTER 21

The guy in the booth looked like the sort who got the job as a revenge-hire by a manager on his way out. He was scrawny with an angry look etched into every muscle of his face. Titus was the only one he asked for ID. I looked him once directly in the eye like Titus had told me to and then kept my remaining gazes to the truck's interior and the view out my window.

The clerk didn't say anything and neither did Titus, but I didn't see any law enforcement approaching us suspiciously. When I tired of all the views in the truck and the little that was visible outdoors in the snowy dark, I turned back to the clerk who was still examining Titus's ID like there was a secret code hidden on it somewhere.

"Some weather, huh?" the clerk said.

"Freezing my ass off tonight," Titus said. "Supposed to be in the fifties by tomorrow."

The clerk looked back down at the ID and stared at it even more intently. I wondered if that little conversation was some kind of pass code for my entry back into the country. Was this the person on the other end of the text messages sent from the disposable phone? My right leg was tapping belligerently against the truck's passenger door as on outlet for energy I had no other outlet for. The clerk took his eyes away briefly to look out the window behind him then looked back at Titus.

This was it. The moment of truth.. The clerk handed the ID back and smiled. I let out a growly sigh from both my nose and mouth that drew a glare from Titus. Posey had fallen back asleep.

"Seems kind of late to be crossing the border," the clerk said.

"Started at the casino with a hundred bucks and a plan for early departure," Titus said, shrugging nonchalantly. "Screwed the pooch on both."

The clerk turned his eyes to me and then he looked back at Titus again. I had to turn my brain off because thinking about things not to do to bring attention to myself was driving me crazy enough to possibly bring attention to myself. So I didn't think about anything.

"Welcome back," the clerk finally said.

I didn't let my breath out until we were clear of the customs plaza and on our way over the bridge. Then I was giddy. I'd made over the border twice without running into trouble and was really no worse for the wear. Sure I'd been shot at, but I wasn't hit and I wasn't as sore as I'd been after two car accidents. I'd also been able to nap which had recharged not only my body but my mental faculties. I was still surprised when we passed by the outhouse and Titus pulled off to the side of the road.

"I feel like I've said this more to you than I've said anything to anyone ever," Titus said. "Get out."

"You can't park on the side of the bridge. A cop is going to stop us and—"

"No. Get out."

I looked back to Posey who just stared past me. I don't know that she would have been much of an advocate for me anyway.

"Why all the effort to get me across the border only to—"

"Now," he said. "You're already late."

I got out of the truck because I didn't want to be dragged out, which I was sure Titus would do if I resisted. Another car approached us from the opposite direction and made a rough U-turn over the median and pulled in behind Titus's truck. When I saw Lindsey get out of the passenger side of the new car, I was finally ready to give up. I began looking for the best way to get to the bridge railing so I could jump.

Lindsey got into Titus's truck where I'd just been sitting and they pulled away. The other car flashed its headlights at me but I didn't move. There wasn't enough traffic on the bridge to make suicide by car a viable alternative to jumping off the bridge so I stayed where I was until the driver got out the new car. When I saw who it was, I immediately regretted not jumping.

"Do you know what it feels like to wake up after a Taser attack?" Rickard asked.

"I was thinking about jumping into the water," I said. "But there's actually some good that can come of this meeting."

"I want to cut your heart out and feed it to a tiger I keep in Lakeland. That's in Florida where the Tigers have spring training."

"I'm going to walk to you as a show of good faith," I said, taking two short steps toward his car. "Maybe you can wait to murder me until after we chat."

I made it to his car before Junior spoke again. He was walking toward the passenger side with me and I thought he was going to punch me. Instead he said, "You drive. This bridge scares the shit out of me."

"That was some U-turn," I said, pulling back out onto the bridge. "You took it at just the right —"

"You remember where I live right?"

"How did you get out of Lindsey's trunk?"

"You want to this soap opera style, all dramatic with a booming voice saying 'last week our hero was stuck in the trunk of a bitch cop's trunk, will he be able to escape before she shoots him?'"

"You're not the hero of this soap opera," I said.

"Drive to my place. Wake me up if you get lost."

I didn't get lost and pulled into the Viking Motel lot without incident fifteen minutes after we exited the bridge. The car stank like cigar smoke and body odor so I rolled down my window and took a breath of fresh Detroit air. Rickard was still asleep and I wasn't keen on waking him up yet. I had a quick thought of dumping him at his house again and stealing the car, but it was becoming quite clear that every person I came into contact with had some kind of cosmic bungee cord attached to them, and if I screwed them over they would eventually bounce back to me. So, no dumping.

When I started at the local community college right out of high school, I hadn't quite pinned down the path my writing career would take and I was still thinking the theater might play some role in it. In order to get a better feel for actors and how to write for them, I took an acting seminar. The section that stuck with me the most was the one on improvisation. The motto for the class was "always say yes".

The scenes always worked better if the actors just went with the crazy stuff happening around them instead of trying to force the scene into what the actors wanted to play. I'd already figured out my life wasn't strapped to any particular story arc, so why not always say yes? I took another deep breath outside, and wasn't surprised to find the temperature had settled in again to a mild degree.

My eyes were watering from allergies when I honked the horn to wake up Rickard. He snorted with his mouth and swatted at me but didn't wake up. I didn't want to stay in the parking lot any longer so I got out of the car and popped the door open with little effort. The apartment seemed even more squalid and depressing than it had the last time and I guessed that was because Rickard had spent some time there recently doing whatever sort of things made an apartment reek of bleach and greasy sweat. When I first caught wind of the bleach smell, my thoughts went immediately to the body in Rickard's trunk the first time I rode with him. That led me to thoughts of the woman who took the body off our hands. The woman who had our money and my backpack with the thesis form. I sat on the couch at the center of the room for a full ten minutes before I went back out to the car and smacked on Rickard's window to wake him up.

"The woman who took that body and the money from us," I yelled through the window because he wouldn't roll it down, "I want to go find her."

He was looking at me but wasn't putting the window down.

"A favor, really?"

"We probably need to get the money. For whatever you're doing in Toledo. Right?"

He rolled the window down halfway.

"Toledo, yeah," he said. "There's a guy who owns a bookstore but his family business is a machine shop with a giant grinder. Big ass thing that could eat a car. Or a body."

"Okay."

"We'll pick the bitch up on the way."

"Okay."

"You still ride in the back."

CHAPTER

22

We drove until we came to an industrial railroad area off of I-75 near the old Michigan State Fairgrounds.

"Look at that carwash across the street," I said. "They have a payment plan. How does that work exactly? If you miss a payment, do big thugs show up with mud and grease to dirty your car in retaliation?"

We got back into the car and pulled back out the way we came. He stopped at a strip club called The Booby Trap we'd passed coming into the area and pulled around back. The van was parked sideways in front of a solid looking metal door in the middle of the building.

"Are you okay for this?" I asked him. "You don't seem right."

I should have been happy he wasn't right because he seemed more like a stoner than the creepy serial murderer I suspected him to be. But I was looking for stability anywhere

I could find it, even if it was in the personality of a brain rot like Rickard.

"It's little probes that shoot into your body," he said. "Most people don't know that. They hook in your skin and pump the juice right into your goddam muscles."

I assumed he was talking about the Taser Lindsey hit him with.

"Should we go take a look at the van?"

"Not without her. No telling what she got hiding in there."

"Maybe wedding dresses," I said.

And stoner Rickard was then immediately replaced by murderous Rickard who grabbed me by my cheeks and pulled me to within atomic spaces of his own face.

"Wedding dresses are beautiful for a variety of occasions and situations," he said.

"Also great for threats to unsus—"

He shoved me against the door and then dragged me forward again so my gut bounced off of the center console of the car. The only thing preventing me from throwing up was the gravity generated by him bouncing me in all manner of fashions off of the interior of his roomy old sedan. I choked down the first wave of vomit but when he pulled a gun from his pants at put it to my head I let it all go. Most of it splashed off of the center console up into my face but enough of it got on Rickard to make him mad enough to punch me in the chest with the gun.

"Goddam it, stop making me do that," he said, wiping his legs off with the arm of his nylon jacket. "I need you straight right now."

I grunted and looked away from him. He put the gun in his pants and opened the top of the center console and pulled out a new pack of Elmo wipes and cracked it open. His upper body twitched and his eyes snapped open like window shades in the morning of a coffee commercial. Last time he told me there was no significance to the Elmo wipes but this performance put that to rest. It also gave our true purpose at the bar, and the fact that he needed me straight, a new interpretation.

I'd stupidly assumed he needed a grinder to dispose of the body he already had lying about, but then he'd said when we dumped it with the cripple lady that she was going to take care of it. So if she took care of the first body, that meant we were most likely at the bar to get the money from her and, in the process, make a new body. I hadn't been hit, and crushed, and threatened enough to fry the parts of my brain responsible from keeping me away from shit like that but I was foggy enough in my moral guidelines that I thought I could follow him into the bar and keep him honest. He took three wipes from the Elmo pack and slid them into a sandwich baggie and put the baggie in his back pocket.

• • •

THE BOOBY Trap had no charm beyond its mildly amusing

name. The building was roughly the size of a narrow hotel room, with a small stage without a pole. It could have just as easily been used for karaoke or dinner theater. There was a bar with two taps and a small grill at the other end. The nude women were nowhere to be seen, but the smell of over-perfumed flesh and self-tanning lotion hung in the air where smoke would have been before the state smoking ban.

There were no tables in the traditional sense, but along each wall were a series of tall chairs set against outgrowths of wood molding wide enough to set a pint glass and a burger plate on. Our crazy friend in the wheelchair was next to the bar, spinning her chair in circles. Before we went any further into the bar I put my hand on Rickard's shoulder and tried to stop him so I could talk to him. He dropped to a crouch and rolled his legs around in a poor imitation of a roundhouse kick that cracked my shins and sent be wobbling backward.

"Oh," he said when he saw me against the wall. "You probably shouldn't do that."

"I never got her name last time. The one in the wheel chair."

He turned away from me toward the bar and yelled at the woman.

"Hey, old lady, what should our friend from the van call you?"

Her chair stopped spinning after another rotation and I noticed she was topless in her chair.

"Call me for a lap dance is what he can call me."

She rolled her chair to the middle of the bar and made another couple revolutions.

"Bitch likes the weed for her muscles," Rickard said to me. "Call her Ma. Keegan's her last name, but we all call her Ma mostly 'cause we hate her."

"Like my titties? Wanna buy me a drink?"

"Uh..."

"He's not so good with the words if he's not at the typewriter," Rickard said to the woman. "What are you drinking?"

She held her glass up and said, "The red stuff that tastes like Skittles and gasoline."

Rickard went behind the bar and poured another glass of the red stuff from a faded gallon milk jug and took two brown bottles from under the counter and handed one to me.

"There's an office behind the bar," he said. "With privacy."

Ma looked off toward the back of the bar and frowned. She took a long drink of her red stuff then slowly rolled her chair to the back of the bar and waited for Rickard to go in first. He didn't and eventually she relented and went in first. Rickard pulled the three Elmo wipes in the baggie out of his pocket and then the gooey bloody knife I'd seen him with at the Tiger Stadium field.

"Watch the bar would ya?" he said. "This will be quick."

I didn't want to listen, but there was nothing else in the bar to keep my attention. There was a mushy crunch that sounded like a punch. Instead of screams I heard grunts and more slapping sounds. I wondered if it was possible that instead of killing her he was having sex with her. Then I figured if he was as broken as I thought, he wouldn't have a problem doing both. I didn't have to think about it anymore when I was joined by a tall, ropey black man in a dingy black suit. He didn't seem to think it strange to see a new white kid behind the bar, which made me wonder if he was part of Rickard's plan. I wasn't going to play my hand though and waited for him to speak. He didn't. He came around the back of the bar and was going to open the back door when I put up my arm to stop him.

"Can I get you a glass of red stuff?" I asked.

He leaned over my arm and knocked on the door without saying anything to me. His body was deceptively solid and out intense pressure on my arm. I didn't want to let loose and give up ground in the standoff.

"If you have a seat out in the bar I'll get you a drink and maybe find something to put on the grill over there."

He leaned away from my arm and my body clenched waiting for a kick or punch to move me out of the way. It didn't come. The man in the grimy black suit went back into the main part of the bar and sat down in the chair closest to the bar. I kept my arm low behind the bar so I could massage the cramps from my muscles.

"Did you want that drink?" I asked. "Or did you come to see some titties?"

"Please, no nudity."

"Seems like the wrong place to be pleading that case. You saw the sign out front right?"

"Place still has a water tap doesn't it?"

"You'd like some water? Tap water?"

I took a glass that looked clean from the bar and filled it with tap water. Then I had a thought.

"That's not slang for a new drink or anything?"

"Just water please."

I gave him the glass of water and went back to my new spot as the bartender. There were no TVs anywhere that I could see, but there was a small radio on the bar that I turned on. A sports talk radio show was on and it was entertaining enough to keep on and break the depressing silence of the bar. As callers nattered on about the up and down state of Detroit sports, I looked around the bar and wondered what it was exactly and what I was doing there. The sun was starting to come up through the city and it wasn't odd for a bar, tittie or otherwise to be closed at that hour, but it seemed like an odd place for a meeting of the sort Rickard was planning. The black gentleman in the suit only confused me more.

"I'm trying to figure out if we're closed or not," I said. "Can you help?"

"You gonna charge me for this water?"

"I don't think so."

He nodded and that was supposed to be my answer I guessed. After everything else that had happened that day, this was so strange because nothing was happening. At least nothing that was going on where I could see it. I suppose that's what had bothered me as much as anything. I wasn't the center of attention in this section of the narrative. That was unacceptable considering what I'd been through so I went to the door and was about to open it when I heard the man in the suit cough.

"Open or closed," he said, pointing a revolver at me. "You don't go in that room."

Before I could make a stupid comment that would have most likely escalated things to a nasty level, the office door opened and Rickard came out tucking his shirt back into his pants.

"Sorry about the time," he said to the man in the suit. "I got a little carried away."

The man in the suit went back into the office and shut the door.

"A few more minutes and we can leave," Rickard said.

"What was...I don't even know...Who—"

"He's giving her last rites before I finish. Then we can get her to Toledo."

I again tried to verbalize the tangle of thoughts in my head without success. The only thing I could manage to do was get back to the bar and drink a slug of the red stuff which tasted as awful as Ma made it sound. I coughed some of it back up and spit it into the sink.

"I asked you last time about the Elmo wipes," I said.

"It's not what you think."

"The only part I don't understand is the guy back there in the suit."

"Preacher," Rickard said. "He had a special something with the old bitch."

"You are a murderer then?"

"In a few minutes, sure."

"A serial killer?"

"Labels. Whatever. I do what I need to do."

"And me?"

"I got shit to do this week. I can't be giving in to every itch and craving to knife a bitch," he said. "After this one, you're gonna keep me out of trouble."

"What about the preacher?"

"One time shot. We have an agreement."

I didn't even know what that could have possibly meant so I took one more shot of the red stuff, which I managed to keep down. That deadened my brain enough to let my moral compass spin directionless while Rickard went in to finish his business. The preacher left before he could help us move the body.

CHAPTER 23

The trunk of the sedan had almost as much space as the old Buick Rickard had been toting his first body around in. I watched as he dumped the woman into the trunk and shifted her around, and then we went to the van where I expected he'd remove the other body but there was no body in the van. There was no bag of money or my backpack anywhere to be seen. If I didn't have that form this whole thing has been a waste. I needed a signature from Parker Farmington to justify the effort I put into the novel and the effort I put into chasing him down to get the damn signature. Without the signature I was a petty thug with no ambition, no future, and a set of colleagues I wouldn't be comfortable working with.

But the search wasn't done yet. Rickard pulled one of those silver multi-tools out of his pocket and started ripping, cutting, and unscrewing the interior of the van. We found the duffel bag with the money, my backpack, and one other small bag or large purse with cash and drugs in it. I was pleased to see him pull the drugs out of the bag and leave them in the van. He handed me my backpack and the other small bag and kept the large duffel for himself and we walked back to his sedan.

"Stay inside the car," he said. "I'm going to clean up."

I didn't know exactly what that might mean, but I didn't think it had anything to do with washing his hands. Rickard went back over to the van and dug around in the front passenger seat until he emerged with two soda bottles and a short length of tubing. He put the soda bottles on the ground and reached back into the van for a grimy undershirt he then ripped in half quite easily. His movements were very measured and methodical and I was entranced watching him until he stuck one end of the tubing into the van's gas tank and the other into his mouth.

I'd heard stories from my parents about siphoning gas when they were younger and when gas prices spiked over $4 a while ago it was on the news a lot, but I'd never seen anybody do it and it made me sick to my stomach. The smell of gas always made me sick when I was younger and even let my mom pump gas a time or two when we went places together so I wouldn't vomit. And just watching Rickard gave me the light brain feeling, the pressure around my eyeballs that signaled impending nausea.

I rolled down my window and had to look away to calm

my stomach. There wasn't much else in the dilapidated surroundings to look at and I had an idea of what he was doing with the bottles and gasoline, so I closed my eyes and reclined my seat and let my subconscious have the controls. My parents made a number of appearances, more my mom than my dad because he was a crumbling emotional tool of a man and my mom was a powerful, if obnoxious and overbearing presence in my life who had so far squelched most of my father's influence. I was too fragile to handle that level of emotional skullduggery so I looked back to the van where the siphoning had transitioned to explosive assembly. There were almost as many fire bombings in Detroit as shootings, and I was surprised they didn't have a Detroit-specific nickname. I leaned out the window and yelled to Rickard.

"If you're going to blow it, why don't you dump the body in there too?"

He waved me off and lit the first of the bottles. After the t-shirt fuse burned down a ways, Rickard tossed the firebomb through the backdoor of the bar then lit the second one and tossed it into the van. Neither explosion was very big, but I knew the van would have some pop when the fire got to the gas tank. Rickard stank of gasoline when he got into the car to drive us away. The nausea came back with renewed strength and I stuck my head out the window again. The wind and car noise only aggravated my stomach so I leaned back in, rolled up the window, and closed my eyes again to see what else my subconscious had to say about my relationships with my parents.

"I should be okay," Rickard said as we passed the exit for the storage facility. "The bitch was good for getting a few things out of my system."

"So you don't need me? Can you drop me off at—"

"I'll be fine until we get close and I start thinking about that creep and what he did to me and how much fun it's going to be to give him his."

"If you're so geeked to whack the guy, why are you worried you might kill somebody else in the meantime?"

"I have no patience and a low tolerance for extensive planning so I'm always on the lookout for an easy out. The last time I finished a book without skipping ahead was...I don't know. It's been a while. It may be forever come to think of it."

"How long until the festival?"

"Sir Titus told you about the festival?"

"The man himself," I said. "Parker. In the context of... well, never mind that. I assume the festival is our point of convergence for your plan. So how long until the festival?"

"Tomorrow afternoon. It starts in the morning; my presentation is in the afternoon."

"I'm not sure I even know what day it is today. I want to say Monday, but that doesn't seem right. With the holiday though that always throws me off."

"Twenty four hours and some change to keep my hands

knife free and those around me alive."

"Then you'll kill my mentor and thesis advisor?"

"Eventually. It's an extended agenda I have for him."

"After he signs my form."

"My reward to you."

I wasn't going to let it come to that and Rickard didn't strike me as the sort to let it come to my expected end either. I wasn't going to let him kill Parker and he most likely intended on killing me at the end of it all, but for the time being on the way to Toledo it was a simple trip with a simple goal. A simple goal that was tested immediately upon our arrival when we pulled into the lot of a motel that made the Viking look like a Super 8. There was only one other car in the lot, a small foreign pickup truck with cans and streamers dangling from the bumper and *Just Married* scrawled in soap on the back windshield.

There were two men unloading luggage from the back of the truck. One was wearing a classic tuxedo and the other was wearing the ugliest wedding dress I'd ever seen, including the one on the Niagara Falls desk clerk. Rickard hopped out of the car and left a smoke trail in the air on his way to drop the man in the dress to the ground. I was close behind, but Rickard was fast and skilled enough that he only needed a tiny window of opportunity to gut his prey.

The man in the tuxedo proved to be an ample advocate for my mission and got a foot into Rickard's groin quickly enough to keep the knife in his hand out of the gut of the man in the dress. Rickard didn't stop going after the man in the dress so I joined Tuxedo to double team Rickard while Dress scrambled off to safety. When the wedding dress was no longer in his line of site, Rickard calmed down and we discussed the situation amongst the three of us without violence.

"It's probably best," I said.

Rickard and Tuxedo nodded in agreement to what they anticipated I was going to say next.

"A place like this," Rickard said.

Tuxedo was the only one nodding now.

"Discretion is best for all of us," he said.

"No phone calls then," I said.

"We don't carry them on vacation," Tuxedo said.

I pointed to Rickard and then myself.

"We're not really the cell phone types on any day."

We then all mumbled pleasantries to each other and Tuxedo went into the motel and Rickard and I went back to the sedan.

"Perhaps," I said, putting my hand on the trunk to stop him from opening it. "This isn't the best place for us to stay for the night."

Rickard swatted at my arm with the knife and opened the trunk when I pulled it away. Then he said, "Has to be here. Part of the plan."

"I don't want to risk the same thing happening later if we run into—"

"This was a minor lapse. You did what you were supposed to but keep your role limited. You're not my body guard, you're not my mother, and you're not—"

"I get it, hands off until the last minute," I said. "You're sure about this?"

"Plan," he said. "We stick to the plan."

Which sounded like a perfectly reasonable idea, comparatively, until a minivan rolled up next to us and I saw that it too was full of men in wedding dresses.

CHAPTER
24

I got Rickard into the motel lobby without trouble while the load of men in wedding dresses unloaded their belongings. The clerk worked quickly for a man with only a passing grasp of what Rickard or I was saying and handed us a plastic key card that had the consistency of one of those fake credit cards I always got in the mail offering to give me a life a luxury for a modest 400% interest rate.

"Is there another way to the rooms?" I asked him. "Without going through the parking lot?"

He said something I didn't understand in a language that sounded like a mash-up of Arabic and Pig Latin, but from his waving arm motions I put together that there was a back exit. We exited and wandered around the back end of the motel until we found a propped open service door that let us cut through to the front of the motel, bypassing the parking lot. We found our room and Rickard sat down on the end of the bed and took his shoes off. I looked around the room on the off hope that there was another bed hidden in the wall or a cot in the closet, but the walls were barely thick enough to support the cut rate artwork hanging over the bed and there was no closet.

"We won't be here much," Rickard said, taking his socks off as well. "And I can sleep on the floor."

"I don't imagine you figured on having guests when you reserved the room."

"Give me your socks."

"Ew. No."

"I've got to go wash my feet...after, you know, and I need another pair to put on."

"You've got a lifetime supply of Elmo wipes, but you forgot to bring—"

"I didn't forget. This is how it always is. To keep my essence in the pool."

That seemed like silly thing to say even for someone as crazy as Rickard and I began to suspect he was taunting me like he taunted Parker with the wedding dresses. He knew I thought he was a crazy killer and he was going to push that impression to the envelope. I wasn't going to be intimidated. What I'd seen that day had toughened me in a way I was quite pleased with because nothing else had really wised me up in life. The single biggest event in my life was what happened with Melissa, and all that had done was shut me down emotional but I can't say I learned any lessons about life or I wouldn't have been rooming with a murderer in an hourly motel in Toledo, surrounded by men in wedding dresses on the eve of a book festival where one of my professors was likely to be murdered.

"I know what you're doing," I said, moving to the back corner of the room away from the door and sitting in the small wooden chair where the phone book and a stack of local takeout menus served as our welcome kit.

"I'm trying to get it right. Please give me your socks."

"You're acting like what you think I think a serial killer would act like. To intimidate me like you tried to intimidate Parker in Niagara Falls with the waitress and the desk clerk in wedding dresses trying to kill us."

"Can I take a shower before we discuss that bullshit you were just spewing?"

"I don't care. I'm still not giving you my socks."

Rickard huffed and put his own socks back on then took off the rest of his clothes and flung them haphazardly on the bed. This was what I imagined his default setting was and all the crap about being meticulous and any efforts at being precise were more of the serial killer put on. When he was in the bathroom and I heard the shower running I left the room and went back to the lobby to see what else I could learn about the van load of men in wedding dresses.

The area around the motel was quiet and I focused on each crunch of my shoes on the snow covering the parking lot. Crunching snow late at night or early morning was one of the first sounds and images I developed as a writer and for a while every story or novel I wrote began at night with someone walking across crunching snow. I'm not normally a morning person. I like to stay up late and sleep in, a schedule befitting a creative writing graduate student as opposed to a white collar wage slave, but when forced to be awake during the early hours, I always enjoyed it. I enjoyed the quiet most of all. It's hard to get the voices in my head to shut the hell up most of the time, but when I'm outside and it's dark and cold, my brain shuts down and lets me have a few minutes to myself. While I walked, I was my own worst enemy. And though my brain was clear of the voices, I kept thinking about my parents, which was something I rarely did even when I was around them.

The few people in my life who had the pleasure of meeting my parents always marveled at how I was able to turn out so normal. For the first twenty years or so of my life, from the outside it would have looked like we had the perfect modern family. Dad was an autoworker living the last phase of the manufacturing American dream; mom stayed at home to cook and clean and raise the two kids, a boy and a girl, in the suburbs of Michigan. The house was spotless, the income above average, and the credit card debt manageable compared to their peers.

But as my sister and I got older we began to see the cracks in the facade and the underlying current of depression, greed, lies, and manipulation. My mother's quest for the perfect family life put her at odds with the fallibility of humans and their general desire to live more like the Simpsons than the Cleavers. My dad's life as an uneducated autoworker was merely a cover for his secondary life as an uneducated con man and philanderer. He went in my eyes from being the smartest man without a degree I knew to being the stupidest man I knew as an adult. And my mother went from being an overprotective but loving mom to a manipulative shrew who used the occasion of Melissa's miscarriage to preach the evils of premarital sex, living together without marriage, liberal universities and abortion, all without a ring of compassion or genuine emotion.

After that I cut ties with them, started my pathetic attempt to live on my own, and hadn't really thought of them much at all until just then. It made me feel good to know that I hadn't seared all of my emotional attachment to my family and that in a crisis I still thought about my mommy. Unfortunately, once there was a crack in that emotional dam, it came rushing pretty quickly. Then I started thinking more about Melissa and the baby and growing up with my parents and all of the good stuff and it was a crushing weight on my chest and I collapsed in the parking lot and started crying again.

I wanted to go back to the house I grew up in and sit in my bedroom and read. I wanted to go back to the warm little apartment I had with Melissa that always smelled like cookies and Hamburger Helper and read in my chair by the window. I'd spent so much time looking at a dreamy future

I apparently hadn't dealt enough with my past. But I knew I couldn't go back, and I knew at some level that in a traumatic situation I was glossing over all of the bad stuff, but it shook me enough to reevaluate what I was doing and why I was doing it.

I didn't want that phase of my life to be one more area I botched and would cry about later when I trying to fix whatever new life I was leading that wasn't making me happy. I was going to do things right and that started with keeping Rickard from murdering Parker. I still had much to learn from Parker and I thought he could help me work through my past family issues through my writing. He'd always been telling me to dig deeper on my characters and not be happy with one-note caricatures. I was realizing then that my personality had enough damaged facets to provide depth for an entire nation of characters.

But first, the plan. Figure out what Rickard was planning. Stop him from doing it. Get my thesis form signed. But for that part I wondered if I might not even need violence. I'd had such an emotional catharsis that I could talk to Parker and maybe convince him to give me another chance as his student.

The first part of the first part of that plan was getting back to the room and giving Rickard whatever he wanted so I could build a bond with him. Even if that meant giving him my socks. On my way back to the room, I saw one of the brides from the van was standing out by the empty pool smoking a cigar, so I went to him first to see if I could learn anything useful.

"I had this neighbor once," I said to him as I approached, "who would always sit out in his driveway and smoke cigars that smelled like they were joke cigars."

He looked over his shoulder at me and held up the cigar he was holding between two long, thick fingers.

"Maker's Mark," he said. "It's the most popular cigar in the country right now."

"What's with the wedding dress?"

"I like to stand by empty swimming pools and smoke wildly popular cigar products. The dress makes me seem less silly."

This was not a guy that struck me as a hired thug or killer's assistant. He was more personable than most of the writers I studied with, but the dress, and the motel, and the van were all a little too much to ignore.

"It doesn't seem like a sex thing," I said. "And nobody on the drugs would have the heightened senses needed to enjoy a whiskey soaked cigar."

He turned to face me completely and rubbed his hands together for warmth while the cigar hung from the corner of his mouth, making him look like the leader of a community theater version of The A-Team.

"The drugs?"

"I spend a lot of time online and hanging with hipsters," I said. "They like to use common grammar mistakes in an ironic sense to show how smart they are."

"They?"

"We. I. Me. Sure. So really, who sent you guys?"

He cocked his head and took a drag off of the cigar without using his hands and blew the smoke in my face.

"That guy you're with," he said, "tell me about him."

"I knew it," I said. "How did Parker find you? It's got to be Parker. He's more into the psychological assaults than Titus."

"These are guys in your club?"

"What club? I've been in a couple of accidents and beaten up and shot at so I'm a little slow on the uptake."

He took another drag on the cigar, this time using his fingers and keeping most of the smoke in his lungs.

"Follow me."

I took the cigar when he offered it to me and followed him back to a room next to the lobby. The cigar had a nice flavor to it and provided a pleasant burst of warmth and buzz to my guts. My new friend in the dress banged on the door with his elbow and took the cigar back from me after I grabbed one more drag off of it. Two guys opened the door and I was jarred to see them in jeans and novelty t-shirts instead of wedding dresses.

"Cam, go get a copy of the last Gold Case book with the big jugs on the cover," he said, waving me into the room.

A thick cloud of the same smoke I had in my own lungs hung over the room and the limited available dresser and table space was cluttered with liquor bottles. The bed was the nexus of a poker game with three other guys, none of whom were wearing wedding dresses.

"I'm Jimmy Bard," my friend said to me, "and this is the rest of our Wedding Dress Pulp Reader Club."

"Readers? You're not here to kill anybody?"

"Cam might," one of the guys playing poker said. "Can't understand a fucking thing he says and he's got a nasty temper."

I understood what he meant when Cam came back and handed me a book and went off on a speedy verbal tangent in a thick Australian accent I couldn't comprehend at all. He didn't need words for me to see what he was trying to say when he flipped the book over in my hand and I saw the cover. There were indeed some huge boobs on the cover, but I noticed the man between the two women attached to the boobs. He looked just like Rickard.

"Can we meet him?" Jimmy asked.

"I was just on my way to give him my socks," I said.

CHAPTER 25

I didn't want the entire group following me back to the room, so I stalled them with stories of Rickard's personality quirks. While it was a legitimate concern, my main reason for keeping them away from Rickard for the near future was a plan that was developing in my mind for the less near future. To stop whatever plan Rickard had in mind for Parker and the book festival, I was going to need a distraction and a group of pulp minded men in wedding dresses could be just what I needed. So I agreed to meet the group for lunch in a few hours and went back to the room where Rickard was mid-shower.

"I changed my mind about the socks," I yelled into the bathroom without entering.

"Leave them on the television so warm their essence."

"I still think you're full of shit, but I'm willing to go along with whatever cockamamie scheme you have brewing so I can get my damn form signed."

Rickard didn't speak again until he was out of the shower and had put his underwear and my socks on.

"You and I have more in common than you'd like to admit," he said, scooting to the back of the bed and fluffing the pillows behind his back. I stood a few steps inside the doorway with the door closed behind me.

"I have some people I think you'd like to meet."

"When you first started writing, who was your biggest influence stylistically?"

"They're all staying a few rooms down by the lobby and they—"

"Okay, no specifics, but I bet when you started writing your own stuff you imitated whoever were your biggest influences at the time."

"I guess, sure. But about these guys—"

"I'm trying to have a moment here. You think I'm trying to intimidate, but—"

"I get it. We're the same. We're not, but I get it that you think we are."

"We're two young guys trying to find our ways. Yours is writing, mine is killing. You're looking for your voice and I'm looking for mine."

That was the strangest thing I heard him say up until that point and it took me off guard and took my mind of the room full of gambling and drunken pulp brides. But I still wasn't buying the moment he was selling.

"That seems like a stretch," I said.

"But what you have that I haven't had the luxury of is a mentor."

"A murder mentor?"

I could hear the condescension in my voice as I spoke and didn't really try to tone it down, but Rickard seemed genuinely hurt by the tone and that made me feel bad and confused.

"Never mind," he said. "Let's just watch TV until it's time to leave for the festival."

"These guys down the way, they want to meet for lunch and they think you're some kind of—"

"I hear you talk to everyone, including me when we first met, about your destiny and your dreams and how being a writer is the thing you feel you were created for."

"And you feel that way about being a murderer?"

My tone was more curious than condescending that time, but still heavy on unsupportive emotions. I was intrigued by the idea of a soul created and destined for evil and no longer thought he was mocking me, but it was still a pretty big leap of logic to put him and me on the same creative path.

"It's what I'm here for. I don't know what that means but that's what I'm trying to figure out. This event is going to be my big project, stretching what I've learned and taking a shot at my destiny."

"Maybe this is just a phase."

Yeah, that's a better tone. Still curious, but now adding to the conversation and validating its existence if not its content.

"When I was a little kid I liked to hurt things smaller than myself unprovoked. I was a popular kid, never bullied, but enjoyed the sensation and could only stop myself when the creature was dead."

"I don't want to have this conversation," I said. "I need black and white, good and evil or my brain will explode."

"Says the man riding the moral fence like a bronco buster."

"Let's go have lunch. These guys want to meet you because you're on the—"

"We're having a nice conversation. I'd like to keeping picking your brain about—"

"This is too much. I don't want to think about it."

Rickard hopped off the bed and pointed his finger at me.

"You told me you overthink everything."

"We are not the same person. I don't want you inside my head to convince me otherwise. You're a loony murderer and I'm a creative artist providing the world an original outlook on the world at large that forces them to confront—"

"What are the most powerful emotions you have to work with as a writer? Fear? Anger? Sadness?"

"I turned away from him and opened the door.

"I said I don't want to—"

"But you can only create those emotions second hand by telling stories."

"We're done. You can find some other—"

I was stopped by a punch to my back that forced every bit of air in my lungs to the surface and sent me face forward to the ground.

"That's pain," he said. "Firsthand. And fear. You're terrified I'm going to do something else."

I didn't have the breath to comment even if I would have had the words.

"If I shot you in the head and cut your body up, I could produce any number of emotions in your friends and family or perfect strangers by what I did with your pieces. Satire, melodrama, comedy, I can do it all and with an emotional through line you can never match with words."

I tried to suck in as much air as I could but the pain kept breaking my focus on breathing. My legs could still move but they weren't moving me in any sort of useful manner. Rickard put his foot under my rib cage and tried to roll me over, but he has much luck as my own legs and after a couple of tries, left me on my stomach.

"You're right," he said, stepping over me to exit the room. "We're nothing alike. I'm so much better than you."

CHAPTER 26

I waited for Morton Taylor Junior to come back and kill me or to pass out and wake up tied to some unholy machine he created for me, but all I did was lay there for an indeterminate amount of time concentrating on every breath I took, wondering if I would suffocate instead. When what must have been lunchtime came around, I heard the group of pulp brides congregating by the pool and smelled the bitter cigar smoke. I tried to holler for them without success and could only hope they were eager enough to meet Rickard that they would find what room we were staying in and come for a visit. I tried to listen to their conversations but my body's every small motion screamed in my ears, drowning out the sounds of the outside world. When he finally saw me, Jimmy, from earlier, came over to the doorway and talked to me.

"How about lunch?" he asked.

I grunted something that sounded like okay in my head but didn't seem to translate very well verbally. Despite his strange fashion sense and lodging choice, the man had to be smart enough to realize something was wrong with me; I was just hoping he had enough humanity or curiosity to do something about it. When he called a couple of his friends over, I wondered if they were going to help me or rob me.

They helped and used arms and backs and legs to get me in an upright position. I didn't tell them what happened and they didn't seem to care. Meeting their hero could wait, they said, and I told them maybe dinner or a snack later.

"There's always drinks in our room," Jimmy said. "Commercial and homemade."

"Weed and cigars too," another one said.

I nodded, didn't say much else of substance, and they left me alone. They were still intrigued by meeting Rickard so I could still keep them in my back pocket as a distraction for later. My immediate concern was to find the little bastard and do what I was supposed to do, which was to keep him from killing anyone else before it was time. If things kept going the way they had previously, all I needed to do was wait in the room and someone else would show up at the motel to shoot and/or kidnap me and I'd adjust my plan accordingly, but I wanted to try and move around to see if I might die or not.

Nothing leaked out of me or snapped off as I made my valiant, yet unsuccessful attempt to get off of the ground. I was able to get close enough to the doorway to use the floor and the jam as supports in my effort to get upright. I ached when I took my first steps forward but didn't seem to pass out even though my head was swimming with gooey warnings that all wasn't right in my central command center. This was one more beating I was sure I'd have to deal with long term, but I had enough adrenaline and natural painkillers pumping through my body to keep me operational for the short term.

The only thing I'd missed more than sleep recently was showering. I'd bathed once in Niagara Falls and that ended up in a bullet-ridden bath, but I needed to feel hot water massaging my body. I needed the kind of scrub down only bar soap and high-pressure water can provide. The bathroom was still hot and steamy from whatever passed as a shower in Rickard's world, and I pushed out any thoughts that crept in about what he might have done in the shower stall and stepped under the spigot. The shower was hotter and more powerful than I would have expected a seedy motel capable of.

I followed the standard male express shower pattern of face, under arms, chest, crotch, and backside. I let the water linger longer where the pain was more acute and finished in short order with good results. My joints still felt like they'd been welded in place and my muscles protested any extended motion, but my head was clear, my stink was minimal, and the abundance of crusted blood was gone. The only way I would have felt even better is if I had fresh socks and underwear to change into. Even the best shower has its impact diminished by limp and sweaty boxer shorts and damp socks.

Outside, the weather had settled into a more typical Michigan December day, with streaks of sunshine through gray clouds and a crisp breeze in the air. It helped even more to clear my head and my thoughts. I didn't see Rickard or his car anywhere around and wondered if he went to dispose of the body himself. I needed a ride and I knew just who would be willing to help and would also be likely to know of a local bookshop tied to a machine shop with a large grinder.

My guy Jimmy the pulp bride wasn't in the room when I showed up, but a couple of his friends were and they remembered me and waved me in. The room looked to be in much the same shape as the last time I'd been there, but the smells were stale, as though no one had been smoking or drinking or gambling in a long time. They had the TV tuned to one of the courtroom reality shows popular with the unemployed and afternoon shift workers.

"Jimmy and Cal went to lunch without you," the guy at the door said. "I'm Ash and they're picking me up a meatball sub."

There were two other guys in the room: a squirrelly, vaguely European looking white guy and a lanky, roughly built black guy, neither of whom spoke to me.

"You guys haven't seen Rickard then?'

"That's what lunch was for. But we saw you got the shit knocked out of you so we figured lunch was off but we still had to eat, right?"

"Sure, of course," I said. "It's been a rough couple days and I need a favor from you guys if you can swing it?"

"Cam's bringing me back a meatball sandwich from this place we went to last time we were here. I've got to clear my favors through him."

A meatball sandwich sounded really good and I wasn't sure what to make of the fact that my appetite was coming back. I felt I still should have been nervous and sick about how my life was devolving around me. Hunger for something specialized like a meatball sandwich hinted that I might becoming tolerant of my current circumstances. The next step down from tolerable was acceptable and then it was just one big mud slide to petty criminal and prison regular. But for the time being, it made it easier to get through the day and I was willing, again, to make long term sacrifices for short term success.

"Where are these meatball sandwiches?" I asked.

Maybe if it was close I could find the guys I needed and get a sandwich as well.

"Cam went to get them. He took—"

"You said that, yeah, but where is the location? Did they walk or did they—"

"Round the way is what Cam said, and I see the van still in the lot there by our window and that's the only vehicle we got here so I don't think they drove."

I took a couple of steps further into the room and tried to engage the other two in the conversation to see if they might be more help.

"Sorry to intrude fellas," I said. "But do you know if—"

"Reason we had him answer the door," the black guy said, "is he's all chatty and such so as to keep anyone stupid enough to knock on the door busy with conversing so they don't bother us."

"And I really do get that," I said. "Under normal circumstances I'm not a chatty guy either; I hate the small talk. But this is kind of a big deal and I need to know where your guys are."

"Cause this shithole motel downtown in this shithole city is just full of big deals that need attending to right away."

"What about my friend there on the cover of your books. You all seemed—"

"We all is about two of us and ain't either of them in this room right now with you. So you best get to backing out—"

"They're here," Ash said from the window. "Cam and the sandwiches."

"That sounds like the worst band name ever," I said.

Nobody else said anything and I crowded the window with Ash to watch Jimmy and Cam make the trip across the parking lot toward the motel. They each were carrying two white takeout bags and I let myself hope they had extra sandwiches I could talk my way into sharing.

"Looking better upright soldier," Jimmy said. "Got a good excuse why I'm buying greasy sandwiches for my hotel room instead of dining with your boy?"

"He's strange, there's no way around that and he bailed before I could—"

"He the one who put you on the ground?"

"He's under quite a bit of stress and—"

"You think you're the only one who knows why he's here?"

I almost bounced right off of that into my own riff of why Rickard was in town, but stopped short when I realized he might have a purpose in town for the book festival other than murder and public torture.

"Like I said," I said. "He's strange and the main reason he's here may not be the only reason he's here…if you know what I mean."

"I've been to these things as the guest of honor before and they schedule your shits for you it's so tight."

"Guest of honor?"

Repeating questions has always been a conversational tick of mine, not out of ignorance exactly but because I tend to be thinking two or three moves ahead conversationally and don't always keep up on the immediate end of what the other person is saying. This time it came back to haunt me in a most unfortunate way.

"Who did you say you were again?" Jimmy asked.

This brought the other two off of the bed and to the door

while Ash stayed by the window watching us.

"I'm a writer," I said. "Detroit State University creative program."

They slowed their movement toward me and Jimmy relaxed his stance.

"Parker Farmington was my thesis...I guess *still is* my thesis advisor," I continued. "I think he's doing something with Rickard too and I'm supposed to be involved."

"You mentioned a favor," Jimmy said.

"Part of this thing I'm supposed to be involved with, and you've got to understand nobody has really told me much of anything and I've just kind of cobbled this together myself—"

"So the favor?"

"I was supposed to go with our friend to a bookstore that was associated with a machine shop but after our—"

"You want Jordan Johnson's place," Jimmy said. "But I don't think they have the machine shop anymore."

"After our argument, he took the car too and I don't—"

"Come on, we'll take you. I've got to talk to the big guy anyway. He and I are thinking of bidding for a writing conference in this area."

"That would be great," I said.

I wanted to ask for more information about the book festival but I thought that would only serve to alienate myself further from these guys and if the guy we were going to visit was as connected as they were making it sound, I'd find out what I needed soon enough.

I was in the middle of the pack when we left the hotel room and I ended up in the middle van seat as well. None of the guys were wearing their wedding dresses. It would help for the distraction if they were dressed that way, but there were ways to make it work without the dresses.

Then Jimmy said, "So you know about your boy being a murderer right?"

CHAPTER

27

I t was easy enough to play ignorant because my confusion put on the same face as we drove to the Hurt Machine Bookstore. It was down by the ballpark where the Toledo minor league baseball team played. Seeing the stadium after my conversation with Rickard in the old Tiger Stadium field gave me an emotional gut check and once again my audible gasp brought the attention of everyone in the van.

"It's the baseball thing, isn't it?" Jimmy said.

"We've heard stories, "Ash said. "About the baseball stuff and the creepy shit. Did he show you any of that stuff?"

I thought back to the bobble heads and how disturbing the visual had been at the time. I didn't mention them or the conversation because I wasn't sure whether these guys were curious thrill seekers, true crime nerds, or something more drastic, so I kept mostly to myself and let them think what they wanted about me. It was completely against my tell-all nature, but I had mental exhaustion and rabid paranoia working in my favor. When we pulled into a fenced-in parking lot across the street from a large, brick factory-looking building, I assumed we made a wrong turn and were turning around but Jimmy parked the van and the others got out of the van.

"This is a bookstore?" I asked.

"Around the front," Jimmy said. "This is the VIP parking area."

I followed the group around to the front of building where I still didn't see any signs of commercial enterprise. It wasn't until we were in front of an entry area that seemed to be the office section of the factory that I looked up to the awning and saw the logo for The Hurt Machine Bookstore and a small neon OPEN sign in the window.

"Nice name," I said.

Jimmy banged on the metal door and stepped back.

"The machine shop used to be around back but it's got ramps and shit in it for roller derby now," he said.

"Roller derby?"

"Hot chicks in short shorts on roller skates beating the shit out of each other."

"Should we go around back then?" I asked. "My guy was coming here specifically for the—"

The metal door swung open and a tall, haggard looking man with stringy hair and gnarled hands wearing a baggy Green Lantern t-shirt popped out of the office and gave

Jimmy a hug. Then he gave the rest of us hugs, including me, and invited us inside.

"Just filled the bathtub with beer," he said.

Bookstore, body disposal, roller derby, now moonshining? We followed the gnarly man up a steep flight of stairs to a floor that had been lovingly restored to its 1940s glory. The doors all had pebbled glass and the ceiling was a patchwork of elaborate plaster engravings. The aforementioned bathtub of beer was against the left wall of the hallway, an old school claw foot bathtub full of bottles and cans. Next to it and down the hallway was a card table full of liquor and wine bottles.

Jimmy and the guys grabbed bottles of Great Lakes beer but I didn't take anything. The last thing I needed on top of the aches and pains and possible internal injuries I had was alcohol-related trouble. I've never been able to hold my liquor well and alcohol is what had gotten me into the mess in the first place. Our host reached under the card table to a small fridge and pulled out an energy drink.

"Our new friend here," Jimmy said, "was asking about your old grinders."

"Let's go into the rec room and talk," the host said. "The writers will be getting in from the airport any time and need this hallway."

Jimmy and I followed him through one of the pebbled glass doors into a bare office with wood floors, a single wooden desk and an old radiator heater.

The rest of Jimmy's friends stayed in the hallway with the

beer. Jimmy sat on the edge of the desk while our host took a seat behind it. He drained the energy drink in one long drink and crushed the can on the desk. I was standing, as seemed to be my new official position, just inside the doorway.

"Will Sam Spade be joining us?" I asked.

"I'm Jordan Johnson and maybe you better introduce yourself and how you know Jimmy here."

"I'm staying at the motel where these guys are and I was out by the pool the other night and Jimmy started talking to me and then took me back to his room."

Johnson put his feet up on the desk and leaned back in the chair. He pulled a cigarette and a silver lighter with a colorful book cover etched on the side out of his pocket and lit the cigarette.

"You're a writer then? Who do you read? I've got some books maybe I can send home with you. And what about comics? Do you read comics? I've got some guys over in the other room who are starting a new—"

"I really don't want to waste your time with small talk when we all know why I'm here and what's going on. I thought you had grinders here and—"

"Jimmy," he said, flicking his cigarette ash onto the floor, "open the window, would you?"

"Come on," I said, watching Jimmy open the window and stay behind Johnson. "You don't have to threaten me. I just want to—"

"It smells like an ass in here," he said. "Threaten, Jesus

Christ. Do I look like a thug to you?"

"It's been a rough few days," I said. "Nobody looks like thugs but everybody's shooting at me and this guy at the motel —"

"This guy right here behind me, Jimmy? You can say his name. We don't have to pretend he's not here."

"He's with Mort's kid," Jimmy said. "Roommates or some shit."

I shrugged, not knowing any words that could possibly convey my entire reaction to that statement. It was in essence a microcosm of this entire pursuit. Mismatched bedfellows, no clear definitions of roles and some shit.

"I don't know what to do," I said instead.

I took a deep breath, ready to expound on that, but let it out. That had said enough.

"I don't know you; I don't know where you're from or what your story is," Johnson said. "But we're family here to everybody, even the fuckups, and we'll figure out what's going on."

"You'd be the first," I said.

"You're a smart ass, I like that. If it's not whiny. Seriously though, you like comic books? Let's go over and have some pasta. And get a drink. You make me nervous with the empty hands."

• • •

WE LEFT the office and went across the hall to an apartment

that was lined floor to ceiling with books in every room. The books and thick, dark red paint created a claustrophobic atmosphere, but each room had at least two doors of entry, all of which were open at the moment so I could see the full layout. I noticed the carpet was threadbare and the paint around the trim and the doors was peeling, which took away a bit from the elegant impression of the place I'd initially had. The crowd was large and certainly violated any number of local safety and noise ordinances, but the energy was infectious and I found myself smiling several times, something I hadn't done much of in the last year. The nexus of the crowd seemed to be the kitchen and as I pressed my way through I saw why. A small alcove was set off to the side of the dining room with a small stove and a sink and slight fraction of counter space. Large pans of pasta and salad took up every available inch of space in the kitchen and most everyone in the group had a plate of the stuff. I'd been to a number of wine and cheese or BYOB literary events, but this was the first in a real home with real food and, what seemed like, real people.

My family was small and disconnected and I'd always dreamed of being part of one of the giant families you see in the movies or in Italian restaurant commercials that get together for every holiday to eat and catch up and air dirty family laundry loudly. This was as close as I'd come in my life to that dream. Jordan Johnson, the strange yet jovial uncle hosting the reunion, steered me in the direction of the food and slapped me on the shoulder.

"There can't be any leftovers," he said. "She's a real bitch if there's leftovers."

I was hungry, but it had reached the point of diminishing returns where my stomach had turned in on itself for sustenance and I was so hungry I couldn't eat. But the cynical side of me knew this man could help me with my predicament and I didn't want to be any part of the cause of his wife being a real bitch. Another part of me saw this man as a comrade and didn't want to disappoint him.

"These are all writers here?" I asked, scooping an appropriate amount of pasta on my plate.

"Mostly. Some editors though, also agents, reviewers, and bloggers. It's a whole community. Nobody really does one thing; everybody does everything. And comic books. See that guy over there by Sean? That's Victor X, he writes for DC and he's working on a graphic novel of *Justified*. Have you seen *Justified*? I think I have the first season DVD in the living room."

He made a U-turn through the crowd and made his way for the first room we'd come into with the giant television and the most books. I didn't follow him because I was stuck in my own thoughts triggered from something he said about who else was in the apartments.

"You said publishers a second ago," I said, not immediately realizing he wasn't in earshot.

I pushed my way back into the living room where he was

digging through a box of DVDs on one of four couches in the room.

"The official set is in the bedroom," he said. "We've been watching it before bed. We don't have cable. I refuse to pay so much for shit I can get a month later on disc, and I just really hate the assholes that run those companies. I had dialup internet access until just last year because I didn't want to…"

He stopped talking and looked away from the box back to me.

"What? Did I do something?"

"The studio sent me a copy of a special screener they did with the TV writers and Elmore Leonard, that's cool. But I don't see it. Let's go downstairs and see—"

"You mentioned when you said who was here that there were some publishers."

"Don't be an asshole about it though. They don't come here to be pitched and they get pissed when—"

"Oh, no I'm not looking for a publisher. Well, I mean I am eventually, but that—"

"One time this guy, who is a real douche, doesn't even use his real name and his pen name is worse than his real name, but he corners this one editor from Little Brown in the airport bathroom in Chicago and pitched him a book that was so awful the editor almost quit the business. He's over there by the record player; see the big guy with the ponytail?"

"That's the editor? He looks—"

"The writer. He still comes around even though nobody

can stand him. The editor went to San Francisco and works in PR or something."

"I thought you said he almost quit the business."

"He did. Then. This thing with the PR, that's new. I think he went there for a woman or something. Maybe the food. I don't know. Did you get enough to eat?"

"I'm looking for a specific publisher but I don't know his name."

"There's only a couple here, we don't get the big guys or anything. But over by the bathroom, see the young guy with sunglasses on? He's the publisher of Moonstone Books. Sounds like a mumbo jumbo self-help press, I know. I tried to talk him out of it. But they do good shit. Dark shit, some funny stuff too, but they're good. Won a bunch of awards."

"What publisher was Parker Farmington working with?"

"Oh hell, that guy."

"You don't like Farmington either?"

"No, hell no. I love him, he's great. Great writer. He comes down here a few times a year to watch a ball game."

"His publisher is a jerk?"

"He's a loon is what he is. You want to pitch him something? I guess that might work. He's a loon, but he does good work for his people. I wish Parker was with one of the big guys for the publicity and shit, but he's a big supporter of the independents and you should see the design they did with, ah, why am I babbling on when I can show you?."

"You have a copy of Parker's book?"

All of the oxygen in my body disappeared and my head felt like it was going to float from my body. I was about to face my greatest fear. The reason Parker Farmington had been steering me away from writing a crime novel as my thesis was that he was writing his own crime novel and didn't want me infringing on his territory. Then I had a more sinister thought. What if the reason he didn't want me to submit my novel as my thesis was because—

"Here it is," Johnson said, pushing a hard cover book in my hand. "It's just a mockup; quite a nice mockup, hand crafted and all, but the final—"

"What's it called? I don't see a title on this book."

"That's going to be part of the finished product, that and the blood they're going to mix in with the ink."

I opened the book to the title page and let out a breath. The book was called *Blood Diamond* and the first few pages didn't read at all like my thesis. They were better. Parker Farmington didn't need to steal my thesis because he was a great writer on his own. Once again I had to face the possibility that the only reason my thesis was rejected was because it was, in the end, not good.

"Wait, who is Duane White? I thought this was—"

"Pen name," Johnson said. "He doesn't want his pussy academic friends—"

"Ahhh," I said. "This is really good."

"There's a novel within the novel that's so bad he must be some kind of genius to write it."

Johnson pulled the book from me and flipped a little ways and handed it back to me open. The title alone smacked the breath out of me, and reading the first page was enough to complete the assault on my good graces. I slammed the book shut and threw it with every last un-athletic ounce of power I had in my body into the crowd and screamed. Then I started hopping up and down and pounding my fists into the air until I had the attention, and pity, of everyone in the room.

"I thought he stole it," I said. "I wanted to believe that's why he wouldn't sign off on my thesis because he wanted to steal it. But he didn't. Which leaves only one reason why he wouldn't sign off on my book. It sucks. I suck."

And at that point I went from interesting freak show to whiny bore and the party picked up where it left off and Johnson clamped his hand on my shoulder again and guided me into the hallway.

"Maybe now's not the best time, what with your obvious rage and all," Johnson said, "but he's down in the grinders and maybe you guys can talk this thing out."

"Who, Parker?" I asked. "I didn't think you had the grinders anymore."

"That's just what we call the arena. The Grinders. Capitalized. All proper and shit."

"Oh right. The roller derby."

"Come on," he said. "We can still see the chicks skating in wedding dresses. They're practicing something big for tomorrow. You might know a couple of them. They're from

Detroit and I think they're about your age."

It seemed too good to be true, and it really seemed too convenient, but sure enough when Johnson took me outside and around to the back of the building where the old machine shop used to be, we went into a small open arena with a wide wooden track running the length of the outside walls. I saw two girls, roughly my age, wearing wedding dresses and skating with each other. Hmmm.

CHAPTER 28

" **A** re they with Parker?" I asked.

"It's all kind of a big connected thing for tomorrow. His publisher is making this big show of getting the blood from the serial killer —"

"Little Mort," I said.

"So he can mix it with the ink for a limited edition of the novel that's supposed to offset the stupid money he paid for the book."

"The great goddam money," I said.

"Cash I heard, too. I think that's supposed to be part of the show."

"I've seen it, the cash," I said. "I held it and loaded it into a trunk with a corpse."

"You still have it?"

"Until a little while ago. Rickard had it. I helped him get it back and then he...have you seen him around here at all?"

"He doesn't like the big crowds for these things but I'm sure he's—"

"Does he know the grinders are gone?"

"We don't talk much like that. Some emails here and there. He's kind of creepy if you ask me."

"He killed somebody else when we got the money. A woman," I said. "He was bringing her body and another here so he could put them in the grinder and get rid of them."

"That's a stupid idea."

"I haven't seen him since he beat me up at the hotel this morning."

"He didn't kill you too?"

"He's planning something against Parker and needs my help apparently."

"Something tomorrow?"

I nodded.

"We need to get him out of here," I said.

"Tomorrow's his big day. He's not going to give it up for your plan."

"This is it," I said. "My original plan has come full circle and now maybe I'm ready to do it right."

"What plan?"

"Kidnapping. I don't suppose you have a Taser. I think I figured that's going to be my best—"

"Did your original plan involve our friend the serial killer?"

"Not intentionally," I said. "Not at first. And he's not

really a serial killer yet. He's trying to find his voice."

"Hmmph. No Taser but we can probably get enough people together to—"

"No more people. People suck. I'm sorry, you've been very helpful and I appreciate it; this place really does feel like home more even than my own home, but I've gotta keep this to just me and him."

Johnson nodded and looked down at the floor. I wondered if he was thinking of ways for me to get to Parker, but then he looked up, waved his arm in the air and hollered for Parker to come join us and he did. I wanted to punch him but I mostly wanted to get him out of there and get my form signed.

"Who invited you?" he asked me.

"There's talk," Johnson said. "Of plans to put you down at the ceremony tomorrow."

"Rickard," I said. "He has your cash and he—"

Parker waved his hand at me and I thought he was going to flip me off but he was just dismissing my presence.

"I know exactly where my money is and what that lunatic is planning."

"And you're going to let him?"

He waved me off again and walked away. I didn't stop him.

"You said his publisher is here too," I told Johnson. "I want to talk to him. He's got more at stake if Parker is killed than Parker does."

"You don't know this publisher. That's just the sort

of thing he'd love for publicity. Author of thriller novel murdered on stage by serial killer from whose life the novel draws inspiration."

I followed Johnson as he spoke to the center of the arena where the largest man I'd ever seen before in my life was holding court with a small crowd hanging on his soft-spoken words. Johnson did the same hand clamp maneuver he'd used on me, but on this fella his hand only made it to the back of his shoulder.

"A word?"

The man turned slowly to face us and, up close, he had sunken features outlined with a red crust along most of his skin. He had a stale stink to him that I imagined came from his mouth as I hadn't smelled it with his back to me. For a large man, his mannerisms were very small and creepy. He spoke in a soft, airy voice which didn't make him any less creepy to me.

"Yes?" He asked.

"This is...ah, dammit what was your name again?"

"Ellis Meeney," the big creepy man said.

"I know your name, Ellis," he said.

Then he looked at me.

"Tell him your name."

"My name is Dominick Prince and Parker Farmington is my creative thesis advisor at Detroit State University."

"You must be so proud of our—"

"He rejected my thesis three times and failed me so I can't graduate because he said my work lacked literary style and merit."

"Oh dear."

"But I'm here right now to stop your opening ceremony tomorrow because I need to save Parker from a killer who wants to—"

"Your melodramatic needs are not important," Ellis said to me. Then he turned to Johnson. "You know of my plans and their broad gestation periods yet you brought me this fool—"

"I'm not a fool. I'm someone trying to do the right thing and I deserve—"

"You deserve nothing," Ellis said. "None of us are deserving of our next breath lest we take it for granted. Creative breaths are even less guaranteed. I've made plans that will be good for many and one fool will not—"

"Stop calling me a fool. I'm trying to –"

Instead of hissing his retort this time, Ellis smacked me in a most girly fashion with his most masculine hand. My ears rang as I stumbled backward. I could see Johnson's lips moving but couldn't hear what he was saying. I chose to believe he was coming to my defense. I still chose to believe that even as Ellis walked away from me. Johnson shrugged it off and walked away too.

• • •

I WENT back upstairs to the party and ate pasta in the thick of the crowd and contemplated my next move. It was quite clear I was not going to get my thesis form signed and I was going to lose my fellowship. Part of me wanted to walk away and let Rickard have his way with Parker, but the part of me that still maintained a measure of rationality knew that even as big of an ass as Parker had been to me, he wasn't intentionally sabotaging my career and didn't deserve to die. My other parts couldn't figure out what to do about it though.

With enough planning I could put together a kidnapping plot to get Parker out of town during the night and keep him safe for a day or so. That would be long enough to foil Rickard's baseball/literary themed slaughter, but he seemed unhinged enough to resent that and pursue both of us to our mortal ends. No part of me liked that idea. When I took my last bite of pasta and I still hadn't come up with any sort of plan that might work, I was ready to call it quits and head back to Detroit and the sad excuse for a life waiting for me. Then an angel in the form of Titus Wade appeared in the apartment.

Just when I'd figured this adventure was representative of the randomness of real life without any sort of narrative structure, here I was in what I assumed was the end game of this particular quest. I was coming full circle with a kidnapping plot for Parker that I needed Titus Wade's help with. I know I was a much different person than I had been the first time I proposed working with him, and I suspected he was more willing to work with me now that he had been previously. Even if it was only to use me as bait or a patsy. I could work with that as long as I could get Parker safe.

I was certainly aware that Titus Wade had violence in mind for Parker was well, but the presence of Posey and Lindsey in the game, I hoped, could be leveraged to prevent murder. I'm sure if given the choice, Parker would rather be worked over by Titus Wade than tortured and murdered by Rickard. And having Wade's violent personality in the mix made it more likely that any rescue plot would involve a violent end for Rickard as well, which would prevent him from seeking revenge for my ruining his moment.

Jordan Johnson was the first to greet Wade as I made my way from the thick of the crowd to the entrance way. Before I could join the two for more conversation, Ellis Meany came into the room and moved the three of them out into the hallway. I followed. Titus was the first to notice me followed quickly by Meany.

"This isn't because of you," Meany said. "He got here quickly. It wasn't what you said. I don't need to—"

"Me?" I asked. "What doesn't have to do with me?"

"This better not involve him," Wade said. "I've had enough—"

Johnson stepped away from Meany and Wade and turned me back toward the apartment.

"Let's get another drink," he said to me. "And where's your plate? Most of these guys are too old to eat what they need to, but you're young and I really don't want any fucking leftovers."

I let him lead me back into the apartment. Food didn't sound very good but I agreed to another drink and he handed me a beer and small bottle of Jameson. I tried to put the Jameson in my pocket, but he swatted my hand before I could and took the bottle from me.

"You've had a rough day," he said, "and it's not going to get much better so why the hell should you have to remember it?"

"Those bozos aren't going to be able to protect Parker."

"They'll do better than you could, or have so far. Ellis has a shit load of money riding on Parker."

"That he'll make whether Parker is alive or not," I said. "In fact, he'd probably make more if Parker was killed because he wouldn't have the pay the rest of the advance and the —"

"Jesus you're a knob."

He opened the bottle of Jameson and handed it back to me. I really wanted to get drunk and forget all of it, but if I was going to end up screwed over, I wanted to see it coming and know I did what I could to do whatever passed for the right thing in this world. That didn't mean I had to be completely sober though. I poured a healthy shot of the Jameson into the beer bottle and took a long swig. Titus Wade came up behind me and punched me in the spleen.

CHAPTER 29

I was in the process of bending backward to down my beer when Wade hit me, so the blow didn't have much of an impact beyond startling me and knocking the rest of the beer out of my hand. Johnson stopped me from bending over to try and clean up the broken bottle and pushed me into Wade. I thought Wade was going to hit me again but he just laughed and smacked my chest.

"Nervous?" he asked.

"What the fuck? Why did you...look at this mess."

"My fault. You're right. I shoulda known you can't hold onto—"

"What do you want?"

"We've danced a bit, you and me, over this thing with the professor but it's time we both shut up and put out."

"Huh?"

Johnson did a surprisingly effortless job of cleaning up

around us with what he had handy, but I noted that Wade and I were actually sort of dancing around Johnson as he was talking about us dancing metaphorically.

"You told me no when I asked for your help," I said. "Then you punched me and shot me and chased me to Canada, then left me on the fucking Ambassador Bridge with a serial killer and then only acknowledged me again when you needed my help."

I took a breath and waited for his response. He didn't say anything, just smirked.

"And it's probably not even my help you need," I said. "I've guessed all along I'm just a dangling worm, I just don't know whose hook I'm on."

"What you were telling Ellis, you heard that from the nut job himself?"

"Not in specifics exactly, but yeah, he told me several times he was looking to make a scene at the ball park. I didn't know it had anything to do with a book festival, but that's what I think he's here for."

"Interesting."

"And you're going to save him?" I asked.

"Save might not be the most accurate word."

"You want to kill him yourself."

"I don't fucking care anymore. I'm old, I'm tired, and maybe my sister finally found a guy to fuck who won't mess her up completely."

"Then why —"

Johnson was done with whatever he'd been doing and rejoined us upright in the conversation.

"Perhaps a move to the office is in order," he said.

We both nodded and I thought we were going to head back to the 40s PI office across the hall, but we went deeper into the living area, through the rooms toward the back of the apartment until we ended up in a small office with just one door but several tall windows, all with nice views of the rather unattractive Toledo skyline. While the rest of the building was almost entirely book and crime fiction related, this office was substantially comic book themed.

Giant framed posters took up the bulk of the wall space and three spinning drug store racks were loaded with comic books. Johnson pulled a bottle of scotch from one of his desk drawers and poured some into three Batman tumblers. He handed one to me and I drank it all in one gulp and pushed my glass back to him for a refill. I had two more like that before I stopped paying attention to what they were planning and crawled into my head with my other thoughts. Plotting anything in advance went against my nature and it was time I gave up trying to force it.

Johnson and Wade had been discussing an elaborate plan, which had always worked against me in writing. Every professor I ever had preached the glorious freedom of research and outlining, but every time I indulged I ended up with overloaded, boring technical pieces without any heart. My best work came from gut instinct made up knowledge, a base information storehouse, and freewheeling improvisation based on the elements given by nature and fate. I was fading in and out of the conversation and hearing enough of it to piss me off while being drunk enough to say something about it with my minimal filters removed.

"Fucking morons," I said, standing on my chair and wobbling to one of the windows and pointing at it. "He's out there. Right now. Let's just grab him and get him outta here."

I moved my finger from the window and pointed it at Titus.

"You're not Danny Ocean and there ain't eleven of us."

"Just grab him," Wade said. "Off the street like thugs?"

"You can do it with discretion, but come on; he's not guarded by the Secret Service. Why do we have to have such a crazy plot? More importantly, why does it have to wait until tomorrow? Tomorrow might be too late."

Wade and Johnson looked at each other then back at me, but neither of them said anything.

"What was that just now?" I asked. "What aren't you telling me?"

"It's a good idea you have to keep it simple," Wade said. "I like that. But it'll wait until tomorrow. Let the professor drink and have fun with his little friends before we rattle him."

I looked back and forth between Johnson and Wade to see if I could get a read on either of them, but the alcohol was clouding my judgment so I gave up and flopped back into my seat. Content I had made some impact on the planning, I fell asleep while they did the rest of the work.

• • •

MY SUBCONSCIOUS, as was usually the case, saw through my own bullshit and that of Wade and Johnson and assaulted my dreams with enough financial imagery to pierce my alcohol and sleep-deprivation generated stupidity and clue me into Wade's true motive for waiting a day to kidnap Parker. I awoke in a panicked stupor and fell over in my chair. Nobody else was in the office and it sounded from the lack of crowd noise that the party had diminished as well. I hadn't noticed when I made my way to the office, but it cut through the master bedroom of the apartment, which was fine during a loud party with a large crowd. Later at night, with lights off and fewer people around, it was more of a sketchy proposition.

I tried to stay along the outside wall, furthest away from the bed, so as not to disturb anyone who might be sleeping. It was a moot action, as when I exited into the living room, Johnson, his wife, Titus Wade, and Parker Farmington were all sitting around drinking and laughing with a cloud hanging over them that did not smell like tobacco.

"They're keeping you here for the money," I said pointing at Parker.

"I stay free," Parker said. "They make no rent off of me."

"Your book money that Rickard has. He wants to murder

you so he can find his voice as a serial killer and he's got your money right now and I want to save you but I can't do it on my own so I asked him to help but he wants to wait until tomorrow so he can take the money too and then he'll probably kill you anyway because he doesn't like you fucking his sister."

Parker stared at me while I spoke without much of a reaction. I assumed the weed had mellowed him out because he didn't have the roving eyes or scrunched facial expressions I'd seen on him in the past when he mulled over one of my stream of consciousness rants. But I was wrong again with my impression of him, because he had been thinking about what I said but managed to keep his poker face intact so I was caught off guard.

"The first time you inquired about Mr. Wade's services related to me," he said, taking another puff from the joint they were passing around, "was that in regard to my safety as well?"

Ah fuck. How the hell did he know about that? It shouldn't have surprised me, but even at my peak of narcissism I didn't think Parker Farmington would put his own safety at risk just to have something else to hold over my head, but that was how it was starting to look to me and it raised a couple of questions. 1) Why? What could I have possible done to this man to justify such suicidal vengeance against me? 2) What was I going to do about it?

"How do you know about that?" I asked.

I wanted to smack myself as I said that, wishing my skill with fictional dialogue extended itself to my actual conversations.

"I was drunk, you were an ass," I said.

Parker took one more draw from the joint and handed it over to Wade who handed it to Johnson.

"Now I'm high and you're being the ass," Parker said.

I opened my mouth to protest but nothing came out. I waved my hands over my head hoping to shake loose something verbal but still nothing. Finally I waved them off and muttered under my breath something about hoping they all died of painful sexual diseases as I left. I sat at the bottom of the stairs for several minutes pondering my options, which seemed, right then, limited to a long future of menial labor or suicide. When I tired of that I went back to the hotel to sleep off my depression before beginning my decent into alcoholic nirvana. Instead I found Posey Wade dressed in a wedding gown and tied to the bed with Rickard standing next to her pointing a gun at me.

"We're changing the rules," he said.

CHAPTER 30

"Sit down next to her and shut the fucking door," Rickard said.

I looked over at Posey who seemed to be alive but quite drugged up. The Elmo wipes on the nightstand and the wedding dress on Posey hinted at a pending murder. But he had a gun instead of his knife, which was out of character for him.

"You have a gun," I said. "Doesn't that violate —"

"Sit. Down. And have some water. There's going to be a lot of talking."

I'd seen Rickard earlier in our adventure handling a gun and he hadn't looked uncomfortable with it, but this time he looked awkward and I couldn't figure out why. So I sat down in the chair I'd sat in before. I thought about taking a drink from the clear pitcher of water on the nightstand, but I looked at Posey all drugged out on the bed and wondered if she'd had a drink from the same pitcher and thought better of it.

"Put the gun away," I said. "I need you as much as you need me. I'm not going anywhere."

His gun hand kept shaking and he glanced over at Posey who looked to be fading back into whatever haze he put her into.

"And she doesn't look like much of a threat," I continued.

He nodded and stopped shaking his hand but didn't put the gun down. He dropped his gun hand to his side though and relaxed his posture. Rickard finally set his gun on the TV stand and was headed to the bathroom before he stopped and looked back at me.

"I'm glad you realize our kinship," he said. "We'll be very good for each other."

I nodded and quite proudly managed not to say any of the number of crass things that were passing through my head.

"You and me, we'll be the dynamic duo of dysfunctional capers," I said, pointing to the gun he left unguarded. "But maybe you shouldn't leave weapons lying about for anyone to grab."

Rickard picked the gun up and looked down the barrel.

"Hmmm," he said.

He pointed the gun at me and pulled the trigger. Nothing happened. Then he heaved the gun at me. It wasn't a very strong throw and the gun fell to the floor in front of me. I spun away from the gun and caught the back of my legs on the edge of the bed and flipped onto Posey. She squirmed a little, enveloping me in the lacey quagmire of her wedding dress, making it tough to prepare myself for Rickard's next move.

"I need a center," Rickard continued. "Too many things are changing and I need a core. You know. Something to — what are you doing?"

He dropped to the ground near where the gun had fallen and picked it up.

"That fucking dress," I said. "Nearly swallowed me —"

"Right. Yes. The dress. Sorry," he said, tossing the gun back and forth between his hands. "We should get rid of this thing. It's not loaded and I'm not even sure it would work if it were."

"What did you give her anyway? I was just rolling all over her and she barely moved."

"This, that, and some booze. She's surprisingly easy to subdue. But she'll wake up angry and twitchy so let's hope that doesn't happen soon."

"You don't know how long you knocked her out for?"

"Back in our early days together she'd have a couple of dive bar long islands and —"

"Together?"

"In school. Freshman I think. Certainly more than four years ago. I think we've all managed to stretch the experience by a year or —"

"What kind of together? Dating together?"

"I don't date. Poke her again and make sure she's still out of it and we'll take our bait to the shop."

"So we're going to trade the nutty bounty hunter's drugged-out sister for my pompous and vindictive professor?"

Rickard nodded.

"I wonder if I should bring my earmuffs."

It took two of us to carry Posey and she started to wake up halfway between the motel and the bookstore. The wedding dress made it easier to keep her subdued but my arms were beginning to fade on me.

"Shit. She's kicking," I said. "I think I'm going to—"

"Drop her," Rickard said. "Maybe that'll knock her back out."

"I'm not going to—"

Rickard was holding the end with Posey's head and when he let go I dropped my end and tried to catch her whole body without success. Instead of just her head hitting the ground, her entire body hit.

"Kick her to see if —"

"This side of you, I'm not digging it," I said. "Creepy is one thing, even the whole murder planning I've made peace with, but you don't have to be such an aggressive asshole."

"Should we get her a lacy pillow then? Would that make using her as bait a more comforting experience?"

The tone of Rickard's voice concerned me and I would

have probably gone deep inside my head to consider the full impact of what I was involving myself in if I didn't see Titus Wade leaving the bookstore with my professor clinging to his shoulder. Rickard noticed too but instead of hiding, he drew Titus's attention to us.

"We trade now, you lumber-headed jackass," Rickard said.

Wade turned to look in our direction while Parker continued walking away from the bookstore.

"What the fuck?" Wade said. "Why are you —"

"This is your sister," Rickard said.

I mentally smacked myself at the stupidity of what Rickard was doing, but I was also trying to analyze the situation and see how it might play out. I got the sense that the end game was unfolding and that once Rickard had Parker he would set forth with whatever his plan was and I was going to have to save Parker before Wade or Rickard could kill him.

In one sense I was terrified because I had no idea how I was going to do that, since both Wade and Rickard were bigger, stronger, and smarter than I was. But another part of me was quite pleased because with those actions I would be moving from anti-hero (possibly villain, depending on who was telling the story) to hero-hero. Wade and Rickard were the villains, Parker was the victim, and I would be the hero. As the hero, I needed to get between Rickard and Wade, who was revving up like a bull eyeing a matador.

"Why do you have my...what is she —"

"She's wearing a wedding dress," Rickard said. "You know what girls do after they wear a wedding dress, don't you?"

I saw my first opening for heroic behavior as Wade charged Rickard. Parker was still walking away from the bookstore and didn't seem to be aware of what was going on behind him. I thought if I could get to him while Wade was occupied with Rickard I might be able to get him out of there without anyone getting hurt. I still wasn't sure about how to get to my backpack with my thesis form for him to sign, but I figured that if he saw me as his savior he'd be so eager to repay me that he'd have the department prepare and authorize another one and extend the deadline to make it work.

As I headed after Parker to grab him, I started thinking more about how resistant Parker might be to help me after what he'd been through so far. If I grabbed him right then with very little real danger in play, he'd likely think it was another kidnapping attempt. But if I let Rickard's plan play out a little bit, enough for Parker to see what kind of danger he was in, I suspected he'd be more willing to see me as a hero for saving him.

So instead of grabbing Parker and taking him away from danger, I yelled, "He's getting away."

Wade turned to go back and grab Parker, but Rickard dragged Posey to her feet and put a gun to her head.

"Leave him," Rickard said.

Wade didn't buy Rickard's bluff and continued rushing him. This was where I expected it to get messy. I assumed Rickard was using the screwy unloaded gun from the hotel room, but he fired one round at Wade's feet to stop him then shot him twice in the chest and once in the head. Rickard dropped Posey to the ground and pointed the gun at me.

"Get the professor," he said.

CHAPTER 31

While I gathered the drunken mess of Parker from the middle of the street, I kept an eye on Rickard as well to see if I might have a moment to escape. Somehow Rickard managed to keep an eye on me even as he took a syringe from his pocket and bent down to draw a blood sample from Wade's corpse.

"Fucking Rye," Parker said. "Fucking Catcher in the...did you know that rye is whiskey?"

Parker punctuated that bit of poetry with a violent stream of puke that I was barely able to dodge. While I focused on keeping my pants vomit free and not slipping on the icy street, Posey resurrected herself from whatever stupor Rickard induced and went after him hard.

She ran at him low and plowed her head into his stomach and swung her arms at the hand holding the syringe. The hit knocked the syringe loose and that distracted Rickard's focus enough for Posey to finish him off. She incapacitated him with a knee to the groin, stabbed the syringe into his throat, then took the gun from him and shot him once in the head.

It was such a quick blur of activity and it didn't seem to be registering with her what exactly had happened. It sure as hell hadn't fully registered with me.

"Fucking rye," Parker said again. This time without vomiting.

I was staring at the bodies and feeling more confused and nauseated than heroic. Parker was mumbling and I couldn't tell if he was angry or confused or drunk. I'd never known him to drink alcohol, and he'd made several speeches in workshop about the perils of alcoholism and the creative personality so I was less inclined to buy that excuse. It didn't really matter why though; he was as useless as I was. That left Posey. The most heroic of us at the moment, dressed in a grimy, ripped wedding dress. She gathered all of the weapons from the street and shoved them into pockets in her brother's jacket.

"Get them both," she said to no one in particular. "In the store."

I looked at Parker who looked like he was ready to fall asleep. Posey waved her arms toward the store so I figured she wanted me to help her move the bodies. The store where they just came from didn't seem like a very good idea, but leaving them in the street for cops or witnesses to find was a worse idea. The underfunding/incompetence/apathy of the Toledo PD was the only reason we hadn't been swarmed by police yet.

Posey dragged her brother with freakish ease while I struggled with the gaunt, yet unforgiving weight of Rickard. When we had them both in the stairwell leading up to the living area of the store, Posey asked me for my phone.

"I don't have one."

"Of course you don't," she said. "Why would you?"

"Parker doesn't have one either."

"Parker believes in something. In the spirit of personal communication and in the —"

"Bullshit," I said.

"You probably just forgot to pay your bill."

"I didn't forget," I said. "It was intentional."

I followed Posey up the stairs, staying a few feet back of the puffy train of lace on the back end of her dress. Parker was behind me and I wasn't sure how long he'd been there but made a mental note to keep better track of him. I was no longer concerned about the fate of my thesis form. I was concerned with the number of people around me being violently and quickly murdered. Ellis Meany met us at the top of the stairs, bitching about the noise outside before he took full stock of who we were.

"Oh, the sister," he said. "Has your brother taken a pause in his menace?"

She looked back at me and pointed to Meany.

"Tell him."

Then she looked back at Meany.

"Where's your phone?"

Meany started to answer her, but Posey began wobbling back toward the stairs and he reached out to grab her before she fell backward.

"Oh hell," Posey said.

Then she fell forward and passed out.

"Rickard drugged her," I said. "Her brother drugged Parker."

Meany leaned forward enough to look at the bodies at the bottom of the stairs.

"And who drugged those gentlemen?"

I made a finger gun and poorly executed gun noise.

"Rickard popped Wade and Posey knocked off Rickard," I said.

"We need tea," Meany said. "Tea with alcohol and biscuits."

Meany and I carried Posey into the living area and laid her out on a couch in a far corner of the room. I took a few steps backward toward a comfortable looking recliner and was about to plop myself down and wait for help when it occurred to me that Posey had passed out before she could call. I wasn't sure who she intended to call, but there was only one person who could help with a police problem and a Titus Wade problem. I needed a Special Liaison.

I found Lindsey's card and had Meany show me to a

phone. As the phone rang, I waffled about whether I wanted her to answer or not. I hadn't seen her since she and Wade dumped me off with Rickard in Canada. I wondered what she'd been doing with Rickard prior to the meeting and I also wondered what she'd done with Wade after they left me. After a number of rings I don't really remember I hung up and thought about other options I might have. A few seconds later the phone rang and I picked it up.

"Hello," I said.

Meany appeared next to me, apparently angry that I was answering a phone that wasn't mine.

"Who is that in the background?" Lindsey asked.

"This is Dominick," I said. "I just —"

"I know who I'm talking to. I'm the one who called you back. I want to know who —"

"This isn't my number."

"Is that Ellis? Tell him I'm at The Golden Keg and ask if he wants me to pick him up something."

"Listen, there's been a...something happened to Titus. Posey was going to —"

"I know what happened," she said. "I'm down the street getting...I'm not wasting my time telling you this. Just ask —"

"It's Lindsey," I said to Meany. "She's at —"

"The Golden Keg," he said. "I should have figured. Tell her they don't carry the brand I like anymore but to grab some ice. They have the best ice for scotch."

I handed the phone to Meany and went back to the couch and sat next to Posey and fell asleep. A short time later Lindsey showed up in her full uniform looking crisp and in charge. Posey was still wearing the wedding dress, but her hair had been cleaned up and her face was free of grime.

"We've got shit to do and it's gonna be messy and beautiful," Lindsey said. "But it's got to happen now. Do you have a clean shirt?"

"Maybe I should wear a tuxedo," I said, pointing to Posey's dress.

"You ever try to get out of a wedding dress in under an hour?" she asked.

Ellis gave me a soft black bowling shirt with the bookstore's logo on it and examined my pants closely before deeming them acceptable.

"To the grinders then," he said.

"The grinders? What?"

"A celebration of the life of Titus Wade," Meany said. "Then disposal of the body of he and his murderer."

I looked to Posey and Lindsey.

"You're grinding them up?"

"Fat man there needs the blood to finish his creepy print job and I need as much flexibility as possible in explaining to my friends from the Toledo Police Department what in the hell happened as I tried to save a University professor from a crazed ex-student."

"That's disgusting."

"We'll make it beautiful," she said. "Come on."

As we headed down the stairs as a group, I noticed that Titus and Rickard's bodies had been moved. I figured they'd been moved to the grinders but by whom and when were questions I didn't ask. Ellis Meany was the first out and held the door for the rest of us. We went next door into the main machine shop through a massive metal door that took the strength of both Ellis and I to hold open for Posey and Lindsey. The machine shop was a massive open area that smelled like wet metal and stale smoke. It looked like a graveyard for industrial machinery from the 1960s. Everything was dark green and looked like it had been attacked by sledgehammers and rust fairies.

The bodies were laid out in front of what I assumed were the grinders. All of the machinery looked the same to me, but this machine was slightly larger and had a chute at one end that seemed like it might be able to accommodate a human body. We gathered in a circle around the bodies and looked to Lindsey to lead us, but she was crying. Then I started crying.

"Don't fucking cry Dominick," Posey said, also crying. "This isn't about you."

She was right, so Ellis Meany and I stepped back as Posey kneeled down next to her brother and took his hand. Parker came from somewhere behind me and knelt next to her and put his hand on her shoulder. Posey wasn't sobbing theatrically, but I could tell she was really crying. I imagined little Posey and little Titus playing tag in a backyard and riding bikes and wrestling.

I imagined the dates Titus and Lindsey would have gone on and what weird outfits that would have constituted dressing up for both of them. They could have been wed in a civil ceremony on a Friday at city hall and celebrated their anniversary at a dive bar ten years down the line when all of the traditional couples they knew had long since divorced. And it dawned on me that this was all about the love. Love strong enough to be with a man your brother disapproved of. Love strong enough to risk jail and the fury of your sister to protect her from men you deemed unworthy. Love of yourself strong enough to sacrifice the search for love because you made a pact with God in the heat of appreciation after a tragedy. I took two more steps back because I couldn't think of anything I loved that much.

"I'm sorry," I said.

And then I left.

EPILOGUE

On the Saturday night after Christmas, after another anonymous holiday party I'd been invited to out of pity, I showed up for the third time at a warehouse store on the outskirts of Detroit. I was drunk on cheap scotch and self-loathing bullshit looking to buy supplies for a hanging. It was ten minutes until closing time and I was telling the wide checkout girl in the wide orange apron about holiday suicide statistics. She looked at the roll of plastic and the length of rope I'd put on the counter then she looked at me and scanned it without conversation. I was about to pay when someone tapped me on the shoulder from behind. When I turned to see who it was, I saw Parker Farmington holding a bundle of rope and a jug of drain cleaner.

"I've got a year or two left at most," he said, "and I talked Ellis into putting my money into an endowment for a writing fellowship that will live long beyond me."

"Congratulations," I said, turning back to the cashier. She handed me my items, bagged.

"You should take it."

He put his arm around me and moved me away from the checkout counter. I could see that he'd put his own items down.

"I'm done with school," I said.

"It's a residency position. Plenty of time to write, maybe lead a seminar, and funding for a full year, including housing."

"Thanks," I said. "But —"

"I could use the company," Parker said.

I put my own bag down and went with Parker to a bar near campus where he talked me into sticking around a while longer.

Acknowledgements

When I was in my twenties and dreaming of publishing my first novel, I imagined writing the acknowledgements in a witty, sarcastic tone and not thanking anyone because I had done it all on my own. More than a decade later, here I am finally and man, are there a lot of people to thank. First, my publisher, my editor, my friend, Jason Pinter for seeing the potential in this book and taking a chance on it and me. He's made this first experience even better than I could have dreamed. This book wouldn't exist without the encouragement of J.T. Ellison who finally smacked me upside the head and told me to write this novel. Todd Robinson published the first version of these characters as a short story in *Thuglit* giving me my first payment for original fiction and my first appearance in print as well as showing me there was an audience for the awful, awful characters I had created.

At several different points in the eight years it took me to write this book I grew incredibly despondent about everything from my talent, to the publishing industry, to my wardrobe. There to talk me down from the ledge every single time were Dave White and Sarah Weinman. I mock them because I love them and I also really don't want them to know how much they mean to me. Other folks along the way who provided encouragement, meals, beds, and tough love are: Jon Jordan, Ruth Jordan, Judy Bobalik, Michael Koryta, Laura Lippman, Kelly Braffet, Robin Agnew, Jamie Agnew, David J. Montgomery, Paul Guyot, John Rickards, Frank Wheeler, Maria Wheeler, Karen Olson, Sara Henry, Chris Holm, Katrina Holm, Neil Smith, Caren Lissner, Holly West, Alison Dasho, Ben LeRoy, Patti Abbott, Joelle Charbonneau, Jennifer Jordan, Kathleen Taylor, Danny Rendleman, Shannon Eubank, Melissa Gallagher, Lavonne Bomeli, and SJ Rozan. Particular inspiration and encouragement for this book came from Victor Gischler and Duane Swierczynski who are great writers as well as great people.

Finally, my wife Becky and my kids Spenser, Holly, and Natalie deserve enshrinement for what they put up with from me, only a small portion of which is related to my being a writer. I love you guys so much.

About the Author

Bryon Quertermous was born and raised in Michigan. His short stories have appeared in a number of print and online journals of varying repute as well as in several anthologies. In 2003 and he was shortlisted for the Debut Dagger Award from the UK Crime Writers Association. He lives outside of Detroit where he can be found screaming at the TV during football and baseball season and playing Ninja Turtles and My Little Pony with his kids the rest of the time. *Murder Boy* is his first novel. Find out more (possibly too much more) at bryonquertermous.com or on Twitter @bryonq.

Dominick Prince will return
(probably against his better judgment) in

RIOT LOAD

Coming Soon from Polis Books